KATNISS
THE
CATTAIL

Other Books by Valerie Estelle Frankel

Henry Potty and the Pet Rock: An Unauthorized Harry Potter Parody
Henry Potty and the Deathly Paper Shortage
From Girl to Goddess: The Heroine's Journey in Myth and Legend
Buffy and the Heroine's Journey (forthcoming)
Harry Potter: Still Recruiting (forthcoming)
Teaching with Harry Potter (forthcoming)

KATNISS

THE

CATTAIL

AN UNAUTHORIZED GUIDE TO NAMES AND SYMBOLS IN SUZANNE COLLINS' *THE HUNGER GAMES*

VALERIE ESTELLE FRANKEL

LitCrit Press

To my Grandpa Murray, who knows how important names can be…as does Yardsale Timex Frankel, his watchdog.

CONTENTS

INTRODUCTION

As with series like *Harry Potter*, names have great significance in Suzanne Collins's books, fascinatingly referencing characters out of Shakespeare, myth, and American life. The entries offered here don't just list all the trilogy's names but go deeper, providing an understanding of the characters' symbolism, along with their namesakes and literary origins. There are Roman names and flower names, set as opposites in a world poised on revolution. There are military names, echoing battles in our own history and their link to the battles of Panem—history will never stop cycling. Some of the symbols are simplistic on the surface but more deeply complex. Bread is a sacred food used to save lives and even make a marriage in District Twelve. It is also the meaning of Panem, as Collins named her world after the spoiled Romans glutted with Bread and Circuses. Katniss becomes the girl who was on fire, but she is Cinna's creation, dressed like a doll in the early books. Only with her flame arrows of *Mockingjay* does she truly embrace that role.

Districts 11 and 12 offer nature names: The cat Buttercup; Gale's mother Hazelle Hawthorne and her children Posy and Gale; Rue, Thresh, Chaff, and Seeder from District 11; and of course, Prim and Katniss. Some of the flower names, especially Rue and Primrose, also appear in Shakespeare. All these link the heroes to the simplicity and bounty of the country, filled with the wholesome beauty of nature.

By contrast, the Capitol is full of Roman names, echoing their obsession with heedless luxury: Claudius Templesmith, Cressida, Portia, Messalla, Fulvia, Romulus, Lavinia, Purnia, Titus, Plutarch Heavensbee, Coriolanus Snow. There's Katniss's Prep Team:

Flavius, Octavia, and Venia, headed by Cinna. And there are the Career Tributes with Roman names to honor the Capitol: Cato, Brutus, and Enobaria, while names like Glimmer and Marvel show how valued and spoiled the Careers are. Some characters, like Enobaria, Cressida, and Darius, are named for famous traitors or enemies of Rome, all described by the Roman biographer Plutarch. Shakespeare's *Julius Caesar* offers nine characters who appear in the *Hunger Games* series (Brutus, Cinna, Portia, Calpurnia, Flavius, Messala, Cato the Younger, Claudius, and Caesar himself). Shakespeare's other Roman plays have at least seven more, covering nearly all the Roman character names. Thus Collins casts the traitors from Shakespeare and history against Roman emperors and their allies, building a world that echoes ancient Rome and those who defied it.

It's also important to remember the series is told from Katniss's point of view. Characters have prophetic or appropriate names, but they also have names based on *how Katniss perceives them*. To Katniss, Gale is a strong wind of revolution, willing to blow down all in his path. But Prim is a delicate flower needing protection. Peeta's parents and Katniss's parents, while major characters, never have their first names revealed. Their function in the story is simply to exist and be left behind as their children grow into heroes. Ultimately, Katniss's own perceptions fuel the deeper meanings of characters' names within the series, even as they reflect characters from our own history.

BIG THREE

Katniss

"Katniss" is of course the cattail root, as she tells us. But it is a heavily nourishing plant, important to Katniss who sees herself as the provider for her family. Her entire life is devoted to nourishing, first as a hunter/gatherer, and then as the wealthy Victor of the games.

Katniss plant

Katniss describes her special plant as tall with white blossoms and "leaves like arrowheads" (*HG* 52). Of all the nourishing plants in the world, Katniss is probably the most arrowlike—a perfect match for our heroine. She adds that the roots don't look like much, but are as nourishing as a potato (*HG* 52). Katniss, from District Twelve, likewise doesn't look like much, but she's just as good, it turns out, as any of the children from the wealthier districts.

The plants of the forest are part of Katniss, so much so that the katniss roots give her her name. "As long as you can find yourself, you'll never starve," her father teases (*HG* 52). While this is literally true, Katniss survives by keeping herself grounded—remembering who she is and what she cares for. Indeed, if she can find herself under so many costumes and identities like the Mockingjay, she will survive. Though the Capitol trains its Tributes in brutality, encouraging them to turn on each other,

Katniss follows her instinctive compassion and bonds with Rue and Peeta in the Games. This saves her in the end.

Elizabeth Baird Hardy, author of *Milton, Spenser, and the Chronicles of Narnia: Literary Sources for the C.S. Lewis Novels* has an interesting observation on the katniss plant:

> It is known as duck-potato, appropriate for someone whose sister always has a duck tail...but also as swan potato, wapatoo, tule potato, and, most commonly, as arrowhead, a name reflected in its Latin moniker—Sagittaria (or "belonging to an arrow"; the constellation Sagittarius, of course, is an archer).

The Zodiac symbol for Sagittarius

Katniss' name comes from the Zodiac sign of the archer (the sign for those born November 22 through December 21). Sagittarius, according to Greek myth, may have been the centaur Chiron, a kind and gentle figure known for forest lore and for training young heroes. More scholarly sources link Sagittarius with Crotus, the satyr or half-goat man who dwelt deep in the forest. He was a great musician and tracker, inventor of the hunting bow ("Crotus"). Centaurs and satyrs are creatures of nature and the forest, a link between man and animal, hunter and hunted. For both of these mythic figures, there's a clear link with Katniss.

Suzanne Collins notes that "Katniss Everdeen owes her last name to Bathsheba Everdene, the lead character in *Far from the Madding Crowd*. The two are very different, but both struggle with knowing their hearts" (Jordan). In this classic novel by Thomas Hardy, Bathsheba Everdene is courted by a rich landowner and by a poor shepherd who proposes marriage when they're equals but then ends up working for her. Katniss, too grows up equal to Gale, her hunting partner, but then becomes as rich as Peeta, leaving Gale and

Bathsheba Everdene and her dashing scoundrel, Sergeant Francis Troy

his romantic plans far behind. Bathsheba, like Katniss, struggles between two such different men, one gentle and chaste (Peeta comments that he's never cared for a girl besides Katniss) and one more violent, temperamental, and experienced in romance. After betrayal and abandonment by the more violent man, Bathsheba finally weds the humble shepherd. The romantic pattern indeed seems to echo Katniss's struggle between her equal in warfare, Gale, and the humble baker, Peeta.

Everdeen is also two letters off from "evergreen," fitting well with the plant names of the outer districts. Evergreen pines are eaten several times in the series, offering another wholesome plant in a world of starvation. Like the katniss plant, evergreens are sharp and pointed, in this case with rough needles and pinecones to defend themselves. They, like our heroine, thrive in areas of low nutrition—in fact, the low nutrition prompts them to be evergreen, as losing leaves means losing nutrients (Aerts). These trees appear at Christmas as a celebration of life, as they're healthy and strong even in the winter (and, significantly, even under vicious snow. Or President Snow). They symbolize a new beginning and reincarnation of the world into a newer, better year. Though the world is dark, sunlight and springtime will come again. This is a perfect symbol of Katniss Everdeen, remaker of the world.

Peeta

Peeta, an apparently meaningless word with Collins's spelling, has many homophones, or sound-alikes. "Pita" is a kind of bread, a humble, simple one that's as far from "puffed up" as it gets. "The flat dense loaves" of District Twelve (*HG* 7) might even resemble pita  bread. If Katniss's father, a gatherer, named her thus, and Thresh, Seeder, and other children are named for their district jobs, Peeta's bread name in his bakery family would make sense.

Michelangelo's Pietà

In Michelangelo's famous sculpture, the *Pietà* (another homophone), Mary cradles a dead Jesus. In all three books, it is Katniss's role to nurture Peeta and unlock the gentle mothering side of her nature. In book one, he is dying from a wound in his leg (prompting much literal cradling). Book two, he momentarily dies from electric shock; book three, Katniss must help him through the Capitol's brainwashing and learn to love him. *Pietà* is Italian for pity—in all three books, Katniss must connect with Peeta through pity, compassion, and love to assure their survival. Of course, Peeta is sacrificed at the end of *Catching Fire,* so that Katniss and the others can escape. Many scholars, particularly the "Hogwarts Professor" John Granger see this as a Christlike moment:

> "Peeta," the man of town and "Boy with the Bread," has a name that means bread (pita) as well as a vocation as a bread baker. As a child, he gives two loaves of bread to Katniss that he purchases sacrificially (he is beaten for it by his mother), bread which saves her from physical starvation and the eating of which immediately inspires her to think of her "Family Book" and the means to provide for her mother and sister. His bread, in effect, saves her. In a world named "Bread" (Panem is the accusative case form of the Latin word for Bread), I think it is transparent that Peeta or "Peter" is an icon of the Christ, the world creator, Who in St. Peter's church at least, is received as Bread, and Who loves the world and every soul in it sacrificially.
> ("Unlocking 'The Hunger Games'")

Peter was a humble fisherman who became Jesus' first disciple, just as Peeta is the first to fight by Katniss's side and believe in her. Peter may be most famous for denying Jesus when all the disciples were pursued by

Peter with his keys, prepared to carry forth the message of Jesus

16

Romans. This echoes Peeta's own rejection of Katniss after the Capitol's torture and brainwashing. Peter too suffered at the hands of the Roman government. According to legend, he was executed as a scapegoat by the tyrannical Roman Emperor Nero. The Christians were rebels in the Roman Empire, but finally became its rulers, a scenario that plays out in Panem.

PETA is also the acronym for the People for the Ethical Treatment of Animals. For gentle, pacifist Peeta who never hunts, this too is an appropriate label. While Katniss is found gutting rabbits and shooting squirrels, Peeta bakes bread and frosts cookies, providing his friends with vegetarian bounty.

Melark might be a portmanteau (or squashing-together) of "meadowlark," a nature symbol like so many names of District Twelve. The lark is a symbol of merriment and joy as it sings to welcome the daybreak. His last name also resembles "malarkey," a word for misleading speech or foolishness, like "tomfoolery" or "fiddlesticks." Katniss notes how Peeta always makes people feel better: "Ironic, encouraging, a little funny, but not at anyone's expense" (*M* 299). Though Peeta jokes and lifts Katniss's spirits, he's not excessively foolish—but that's what Katniss must come to realize. Before the Games, she easily dismisses him as dead weight, unable to hunt or fight. In time, however, she comes to value him and even his laughter. "This is why they've made it this far. Haymitch and Peeta. Nothing throws them," Katniss thinks as the men joke loudly to distract suspicious Peacekeepers (*CF* 156).

Gale

Some may be surprised Gale isn't named for a plant. In fact, he is: Sweet gale or myrica gale (also known as bayberry or bog myrtle) is a bushy shrub with bitter-tasting leaves. It's versatile for many rural uses just as Gale himself is an excellent trapper, hunter, and gatherer: The branches can be used for beer making, and the cones, for candlewax, the

Bayberry plant

leaves for scenting sheets, the bark for tanning skins. Boiling it produces a yellow dye, or it can be made into a natural insect repellent. Since beavers love eating it, they build dams near clusters of gale and in doing so create traps for fish, an echo of Gale with his excellent snares (Grieve).

The more obvious meaning of gale is a mighty wind that can blow down houses and mighty trees. Gale as a revolutionary is just such an uncontrolled force as he demands the deaths of everyone in the Capitol and in District Two in vengeance for his losses. The weapons he designs are cruel enough to worry Katniss, and are finally turned on his own side as well as the enemy. As an unrestrained gale, he harms both sides in the war.

Granger has a different take on the wind connection with his name:

> Gale, the man of the woods, free and unbound except for his family obligations, is an embodiment of Nature, a "gale force wind" of spirit and the experience of natural beauty. His relationship with Katniss is platonic despite their spending years in each other's company and both leading lives deprived of touch and love. He fosters rather than challenges Katniss's purity, freedom, and individual strength or identity. ("Unlocking 'The Hunger Games'")

Further references to the name Gale appear in military history. It's not a surprise that there are many military names in the book, as Suzanne Collins heard much about the armed forces in her youth. As she explained in an interview:

> My father was career Air Force. He was in the Air Force for 30-some years. He was also a Vietnam veteran. He was there the year I was six. Beyond that, though, he was a doctor of political science, a military specialist, and a historian; he was a very intelligent man. And he felt that it was part of his responsibility to teach us, his children, about history and war...If you went to a battleground with my father, you would hear what led up to the battle. You would hear about the war. You would have the battle reenacted for you, I mean, verbally, and then the fallout from the battle. And having been in a war himself and having come from a family in which he had a brother in World War II and a father in World War I, these were not distant or academic questions for him. (Margolis)

Humphrey Gale was Chief Administrative Officer of Lieutenant General Dwight Eisenhower's Allied Forces Headquarters (AFHQ) during World War II. The British and American administrative systems differed so greatly that separate AFHQ organizations had to be established. Gale's job, which Eisenhower called "unique in the history of war," was to coordinate the two (Playfair et al.). Katniss is used to the life-or-death struggle of the Hunger Games but not to District Thirteen's army training or command system. Gale is the one to manage a grieving Katniss and help her present her demands to President Coin as he becomes liaison between the two worlds.

General Sir Richard Nelson "Windy" Gale learned enough from his ordeal in fighting World War I to challenge military thinking of the time and try to revolutionize procedures during World War II. With a suspicion of firepower-led operations, he argued for more stealth training and insisted on mobility and surprise on the battlefield (Dover 28-54). Gale Hawthorne often challenges the organizers at District Thirteen using the pain he endured at the bombing of District Twelve and his hunting knowledge to find better ways to fight. It is his plan that vanquishes District Two, and he eagerly joins Katniss's stealth mission to assassinate Snow.

For his last name, the hawthorn is a thorny shrub in the rose family. It is called *Crataegus Oxyacantha* from the Greek *kratos*, meaning hardness (of the wood), *oxcus* (sharp), and *akantha* (a thorn) (Grieve). A "hard, sharp thorn" is a good description of Gale himself, especially for Katniss who must deal with his anger and stubbornness in the later books. Its wood is very hard and resistant to rot, marking it formidable and well-defended, also like Gale. The hawthorn root-wood makes the hottest wood-fire known (Grieve). Gale's fire for survival, and especially for revolution, indeed burns hotter and stabs more sharply than everyone around him. Gale is willing to kill their spies and allies, civilians, and even himself to win the war, as he announces in District Two, crying, "Bring on the avalanches!" (*M* 205).

> Every shepherd tells his tale
> Under the hawthorn in the dale.
> -John Milton, L'Allegro

The hawthorn was not only a country bush favored by the rural farmers of England and Ireland—it was one of the Three Sacred Trees beloved by fairies (oak and ash being the others). These three trees combine to make magic, rather like the threesome who become the heroes of Panem. As a

Hawthorn blossoms

fairy tree, the hawthorn carries many superstitions—harming the tree leads to death, but those who care for nature will be rewarded by the fairies. Those who destroy Gale's home find themselves caught in the fury of his retribution with savage fighting and deadly traps. There's also a belief that if all the hawthorn bushes are torn up, all goodness will leave the land and that hawthorn bushes cause lightning storms (Watts 180-183). As Gale and his family leave District Twelve behind, it's indeed destroyed by a firestorm. Finally, carrying its thorns leads to a bountiful fishing trip or cows that produce more milk. For Katniss too, bringing Gale gets her a much greater harvest.

The hawthorn was sacred to Hymenaeus, the Greek god of marriage, who was often seen carrying a brimming basket of nuts & fruits. In myth, he never wed, but always blessed the hero's and heroine's marriage to each other, a reference that hints at the trilogy's end (Shepard 245). The hawthorn has also been regarded as the emblem of hope, back to the worship of the Roman goddess Flora, mistress of flowers and life. Following this, there's a tradition that hawthorn branches were Jesus' crown of thorns.

Hymenaeus, god of marriage

At the same time, some country villagers believe hawthorn blossoms still bear the smell of the Great Plague of London, thanks to their aroma of decomposition (Grieve). The bushes are associated with death and graves, as the unlucky thorns were said to spring from dead men's dust (Watts 181). In Teutonic ritual, funeral pyres were made of hawthorn so its smoke could guide souls to the afterlife. Gale, of course, guides his friends from the ashes of District Twelve to a new life in District Thirteen. This mixture of hope, peace for mankind, and death fits Gale's role in the story, as his best friend Katniss watches him grow from protector of her family to a leader of the revolution to a willing murderer of civilians.

THE NAMES OF PANEM

Alma Coin

The most obvious "Alma" is the Battle of Alma, the first battle of the Crimean War. The British and French had a plan to defeat the Russians by distracting them with such an obvious attack that they would fail to notice the true danger. In the midst of the fighting, a cry of *"Do not fire! They are French"* as the Russians attacked threw the battle into confusion (Russell 154). Both Katniss's own distracting attack with her small Mockingjay command disguised as Capitol civilians and President Coin's bombing of the civilian children have a similar effect. Despite these alarming moments and possible friendly fire, the Battle of Alma became a glorious victory for the British and French, so much so that "Alma" as a girls' name became popular as a result. So too Katniss and President Coin have a glorious victory. But all wars, even triumphs, have a painful cost.

Lady Butler - *Scots Guards saving the Colours at Alma*, 1854

Alma also means "nourishing" or "guiding spirit" in Latin, creating the phrase "Alma mater," or nourishing mother, to describe one's university (Hanks and Hodges 12). Alma Coin is indeed the guiding spirit and mother of the revolution, as Katniss is its heroine. But as Katniss discovers, Alma Coin is more of an evil stepmother, willing killer of children in the war and in the new Hunger Games she proposes.

V. Arrow, author of "A Complete Etymology of Names in Panem," notes:

> While the most obvious meaning for Coin is...well, coins, cash, money...COIN is also a military abbreviation [for] counter-insurgency operations. Given Collins' military background and the role that Coin plays in the world of Panem, this is the more likely derivation of President Coin's surname.

Counter-insurgency means destroying a revolution. This seems an odd name for the rebel leader, who would more fittingly be the voice of the insurgency. However, Katniss secretly comes to realize that Coin's mission opposes the rebellion Katniss believes in—as Coin craves the presidency and condemns more children to death in the Hunger Games, she has become the new face of the Capitol.

Annie Cresta

Many characters have classic American names or nicknames: Annie, Johanna, Bonnie, Martin. Among these, Annie means grace or favor (Hanks and Hodges 21). Annie's "favored" status actually comes from her loved ones like Mags and Finnick, who willingly sacrifice themselves to protect her. The birth of her child is another grace—a single moment of joy in Katniss's grief at series end. Annie, a nickname like Delly or Prim, is the childish form of the name, making Annie seem like a younger character. Katniss thinks of Annie as she does Prim, a childlike sister needing protecting. In *Catching Fire,* Mags volunteers for the Quarter Quell to save Annie and thus provides another connection between

Annie and Prim. Since Annie's District is on the coast, her last name likely refers to the crests of waves.

Atala

Head Trainer of the Tributes and likely loyal to the Capitol. Her name may be short for the mythic warrior woman Atalanta. Atalanta's name was derived from the Greek word *atalantos*, meaning "equal in weight" ("Atalanta"). In other words, she could do everything a man could from archery to footraces. Like Commander Paylor's name, this reference echoes the theme of women's equality in battle: Katniss is the greatest of many strong women in the series from Alma Coin to Glimmer. Interestingly, *Atala* is the title of an 1801 novella by François-René de Chateaubriand that described Native Americans as endearing and primitive, rather like the Capitol's racist and demeaning view of the districts. Panem's Atala likely shares these views.

Doctor Aurelius

Marcus Aurelius was a Roman Emperor a century after Julius Caesar. His book *Meditations* was one of the most important Stoic texts, suggesting how to stay calm even in the midst of conflict while devoting oneself to duty and serving others. All of this reflects the District Thirteen doctor who helps Peeta and the other brainwashing victims overcome their programming. His Roman name suggests he once lived in the Capitol.

Avox

Along with Lavinia, Pollux, and Darius, there are many unnamed Avoxes within the series. There's a servant in the first book and a group of them who are killed in the sewers under the Capitol. The word a-vox literally means without-voice in Latin, casting them as the voiceless slaves of the Roman Capitol. In myth and fairytales, silenced women represent those throughout the world who have no say in their lives or political influence (Frankel 21). Vocalizing is a source of power, and singing represents self-expression, especially in the series. The Avoxes have been deprived of all this, just as they have been stripped of their citizenship and condemned to be nonpersons. They represent the helpless civilians and disenfranchised minorities who often die in a war they had no power to stop.

Beetee

Beetee is "Derived from BtU, or the unit of measurement traditionally associated with energy" (Arrow). He and Wiress make a strong team with the telling nickname of "nuts and volts." Volts are a measurement of electricity, Beetee's specialty, and Katniss must watch in puzzlement as Beetee clutches his spool of wire through the Games. But in the Tributes' escape plan, Wiress and Beetee are indeed the nuts and bolts of the operation—the essential pieces that hold it together.

Blight

This male tribute for District Seven is killed early in the Quarter Quell when he's blinded by blood rain, then killed by a force field. His name, referring to a drought or disfigurement, seems especially ominous, and thus he's killed by a blight on the land.

Blighted potato leaf

Boggs

The name Boggs has a military sound to it, and there's good reason. Rear Admiral Charles Stuart Boggs fought in the US Navy during the American Civil War, echoing Panem's war between the Capitol and its districts. The Navy destroyer USS Boggs was named for him. Notably, both admiral and ship survived the wars to be retired honorably, unlike Katniss's protector. One episode out of the Civil War became particularly famous. Charles Boggs was captaining the steamboat *Varuna* near New Orleans.

On the morning of the advance he moved up the stream, second from the flagship of his division. Ordinary fuel, he knew, would not get up steam fast enough, and he had the pork, which formed a part of his ship's stores, already prepared to throw into the furnace. At the proper time, it was cast on to the hissing coals—the fires blazed up, and with a full head of steam on, he dashed ahead. When abreast of the forts, he fired his starboard battery, loaded with five-second-shell. "Now!" exclaimed Boggs, "fire with grape and canister as fast as possible," and the frail boat shot ahead, wrapped in flame, and was soon above the forts. Looking around him in the early twilight, he saw that he was in a perfect nest of rebel gunboats, ranged on both sides of the river. He instantly gave orders to "work both sides, and load with grape." Cool, and apparently unexcited, the men trained their guns with such precision, that scarcely a shot failed to hit its mark, while the forward and aft pivot-guns also kept up their steady fire....The Stonewall Jackson, an iron-clad, came full upon her, striking her with a tremendous crash, and staving in her sides, so that the water poured in torrents into the vessel. She was also on fire, and there was now no alternative but to run her ashore, and her bow was headed for the banks....Fast settling in the water, as she struggled towards the shore, her guns kept booming over the bosom of the Mississippi, until the water was above the trucks—the last shot just skimming the surface. Captain Bailey saw with pride how the wounded thing fought, and says: "I saw Boggs bravely fighting, his guns level with the water, as his vessel gradually sunk underneath, leaving her bow resting on the shore, and above water."
(Headley 190-191)

Boggs gave everything he had, risking ship and crew to take the enemy down. The ship sank, guns still roaring and flag flying proudly, but he evacuated the crew with calm military precision, even under fire with flames raging over the deck. Boggs was welcomed home as a hero. His clever actions of throwing pork into his ship's furnace to fuel his ship, his determination as his ship kept firing, and above all his cool-headed bravery as his ship went up in flames but he continued to fight link him with the leader of Katniss's Star Squad. Both watched out for their crew and saved their lives so they could continue fighting.

Bonnie

A fugitive from District Eight whom Katniss meets in the forest. Typical American/British name, meaning pretty.

Bristel

A District Twelve miner. The city of Bristol, UK, was built by digging up the local limestone.

Brutus

Katniss describes the District Two tributes' "eagerness" and "bloodlust" (M 83). Brutus, one of the District Two Quarter Quell Tributes, is no exception. He offers an alliance during training, but Katniss turns him down, perhaps sensing that a man named Brutus should never be trusted. In fact, the English word "brutal" comes from his name. The historical Brutus stabbed his best friend and possible illegitimate father Julius Caesar; the equally cruel Enobaria, Brutus, and their Career allies savagely murder middle-aged mother Cecilia, a seriously ill morphling, the elderly Woof and Seeder, and other unnamed, ill-equipped Tributes. Famously, in one of the historical Brutus' last speeches as he fled pursuit from Caesar's allies, he cried, "O Zeus, do not forget the author of these ills!" (*Plutarch's Lives*, Brutus, 51.1). The Tribute Brutus is the last to die in the final Games, and this quote becomes especially significant as it echoes Haymitch's reminder to Katniss: Brutus and Enobaria are not her true enemies; her enemy is whoever decides to kill innocent children for the people's entertainment.

Buttercup

Katniss's ugly cat survives the three books and beyond—significant when Buttercup is read as the rough, angry part of Katniss herself. As a heroine from District Twelve, Katniss is in a way like Buttercup—scruffy, unfriendly, scarred. Both are lone hunters from the wilderness rather than pampered pets. Critic Steve Barkmeier comments:

> Katniss describes Buttercup as "the world's ugliest cat" with a "mashed-in nose, half of one ear missing, eyes the color of rotting squash." By the end of *Mockingjay,* Katniss is also much worse for the wear. Buttercup distrust Katniss and Katniss hates Buttercup. I believe that this is a representation of Katniss's uneasy relationship with herself. She doesn't see herself as beautiful. She mistrusts any feelings she has towards anyone but Prim. She even questions her motives in caring for Peeta and accuses herself of only appearing to care for him to survive.

As Katniss and Buttercup make peace, this indicates that Katniss is making peace with herself. When they have rough times, Katniss is anxious and unhappy with who she's become. As the series ends, Buttercup returns with the spring just as Katniss takes the first steps to reclaim her life, venturing out of the house and hunting again. Though she screams at Buttercup, lashing out at him as she blames herself for the tragedies that surround her, Katniss and Buttercup finally cry together and reconcile, Buttercup protects Katniss through the night and Katniss heals him and gives him her breakfast bacon, finally loving the wild part of herself that has returned to defend her and love her in turn.

All flower names in the series reflect the rural districts and a closeness to nature. In particular, the buttercup flower represents ingratitude and childishness, a good match for Buttercup's personality (Greenaway). Cats are known for being independent and aloof, solitary hunters who are slow to show affection but who are loyal and protective. Of course, both Katniss and Buttercup are devoted to Prim beyond all else in the world.

Across the world, cats and lions are considered feminine, while in the Bible, the lion symbolizes courage, strength, and power, all traits Katniss finds within the wild part of herself (Shepherd 178). Katniss thinks of herself as Catnip (Gale's nickname for her and another plant name), the one who drives cats crazy just as she loathes Buttercup, her own wild side. And Katniss is the one to invent "Crazy Cat," the flashlight game that drives Buttercup batty. In flower folklore, catnip, when chewed, was said to bring courage, a good match for our heroine (Watts 61).

In the bomb shelter of District Thirteen, Katniss watches Buttercup bat uselessly for a dancing light and realizes she has indeed become the cat, chasing the dangling image of Peeta. With this knowledge, she resolves to take charge instead of letting Snow torment her. In many ways, Katniss is as helpless as Buttercup, both of them carried away from their village house and forced to follow others' rules. But in the end, Katniss and Buttercup both prove to be survivors, able to live with each other's surliness and defensive attitudes.

Caesar Flickerman

Historically, Julius Caesar ruled Rome and tried to make himself Emperor over the republic. He conquered much of the known world and solidified Rome's power over the other countries, suggestive of the Capitol and its districts. For Katniss, Caesar Flickerman represents the establishment, as he's hosted the Games as long as she can remember in his sparkly suit. Caesar is emperor of the airwaves, upholder of the Capitol's tyranny (like the historical Caesar), and interviewer of contestants.

His name may also possibly refer to actor Sid Caesar, known for the show *Caesar's Hour*, which starred many visiting celebrities. A "Flickerman" is a dramatic documentary about someone's life, echoing Caesar Flickerman's job interviewing the contestants.

Cashmere

District One Career Tribute in the Quarter Quell. Gloss's sister. Her name refers to fine fabric.

Castor and Pollux

They are the camera men on Katniss's Propo team. While at first she calls them "insects" because of their camera suits, she soon comes to sympathize with them. In myth, these were the twin brothers of Helen of Troy. Castor was born mortal and Pollux immortal. But when Castor died, Pollux loved his brother so that he asked his father Jupiter, king of the gods, to split his immortality between them. The twins became the constellation Gemini, but shone brighter and less bright on alternating nights. The brothers were known for being united in all things, friends and partners in battle and in life. The second century Roman text *Astronomica* describes the constellation Gemini, saying:

> These stars many astronomers have called Castor and Pollux. They say that of all brothers they were the most affectionate, not striving in rivalry for the leadership, nor acting without previous consultation. As a reward for their services of friendship, Jupiter is thought to have put them in the sky as well-known stars....Homer states that Pollux granted to his brother one half of his life, so that they shine on alternate days.
> —Hyginus, *Astronomica* 2.22

Pollux is the one who lives on, as with the mythology, though he's destroyed by the death of his twin. As an Avox, Pollux represents all the voiceless people who are victimized by so many wars, but remain unable to vote or protest.

Cato

Cato the Younger, like his great-grandfather Cato the Elder, worked to glorify Rome and held several political offices, though his family were Plebian (ordinary as opposed to noble) farmers (one might say, from the districts). His family had a long history of military service, making Cato a type of Career Tribute, hoping to advance through amazing triumphs in battle.

Cato the Younger fought against Julius Caesar, and from there he gets his direct link with the brutal, glory-seeking Career Tribute of the 74th Hunger Games. When he lost his war, in great disgrace, Cato the Younger determined to commit suicide. This grotesque, prolonged death scene echoes the Tribute Cato's as he screams through the night and finally lets Katniss kill him in her first Games:

> Cato drew his sword from its sheath and stabbed himself below the breast. His thrust, however, was somewhat feeble, owing to the inflammation in his hand, arid so he did not at once dispatch himself, but in his death struggle fell from the couch and made a loud noise by overturning a geometrical abacus that stood near. His servants heard the noise and cried out, and his son at once ran in, together with his friends. They saw that he was smeared with blood, and that most of his bowels were protruding, but that he still had his eyes open and was alive; and they were terribly shocked. But the physician went to him and tried to replace his bowels, which remained uninjured, and to sew up the wound. Accordingly, when Cato recovered and became aware of this, he pushed the physician away, tore his bowels with his hands, rent the wound still more, and so died. (*Plutarch's Lives*, Cato the Younger, 70.5-6)

Cecelia

District Eight Quarter Quell Tribute and a mom with three kids. She shares the name of a martyred saint.

Chaff

Quarter Quell Tribute from District Eleven. His name refers to the coarse unwanted part of the grain plant, and as he's both a troublemaker and a drinking buddy of Haymitch's, the name fits particularly well.

Cinna

Lucius Cornelius Cinna was elected as Roman consul in 87 BC. He had sworn an oath of loyalty to the previous consul, Sulla, but he determined to help the people of Rome nonetheless. He worked to increase the rights of the "New Citizens" who had been granted a Roman identity but no real rights. Cinna's determination to help the disenfranchised led to an enormous street fight, and he was exiled as punishment. In response, Cinna raised an army from his countryside supporters and led it against Rome. He won and was reinstated for a time, but finally civil war once again threatened. Cinna was murdered in a mutiny of his own soldiers in 84 BC. His daughter Cornelia was the first wife of Julius Caesar (Bennett).

Lucius Cinna's only real cause was equality between all citizens of the Roman Empire: those from the city and those from the outlying districts. As such, he shares sympathies with Panem's Cinna. He too works for the government but has a hidden loyalty to the people, and finally is killed for it during the revolution.

Cinna's lack of a last name (that we know of) makes him seem friendly and approachable in the world of the Capitol. He makes an effort not to intimidate Katniss, so much so that she feels she

can speak to him as a friend. And he's the one who makes Katniss shine.

In the play, *Julius Caesar*, a poet named Cinna is murdered by an angry mob of loyal Romans because they confuse him with Lucius Cornelius Cinna, one of Caesar's murderers:

Cinna the Poet: I am Cinna the Poet....I am not Cinna the conspirator.

Fourth Citizen: It is no matter, his name's Cinna; pluck but his name out of his heart, and turn him going. (III:iii:29-34)

This callous cruelty, killing someone only because he shares a name with a traitor, is exhibited by Snow as well, who executes and tortures Peeta's prep team and the Avoxes who once waited on him, because they are tainted by association. When the last living Tributes suggest throwing Snow's granddaughter into the Games, they show that this unfeeling need for revenge, even on the wrong person, is a constant part of human nature.

Claudius Templesmith

One of Brutus's soldiers in *Julius Caesar* is named Claudius, but this is likely a coincidence, as there is a far more famous Claudius with a better link to this character. The historical Claudius was emperor of Rome, most known for conquering new territory to glorify Rome and for building aqueducts and roads. He had a particular interest in law and presiding over trials. Claudius Templesmith, as his last name suggests is a builder of the ultimate arena, the Games and an upholder of the establishment, like Caesar Flickerman. The Games are a place of trial and, though not actually a temple, the focus of the Capitol and their way of life. From their beginning, games were linked with religious festivals and the sacred, especially for the Romans. Games are a struggle to win, to discover the rules, to survive (Chevalier and Gheerbrant 414-415). Katniss discovers all this and more as she enters the arena and prepares to be sacrificed.

Clove

At first glance, her name appears to be a spice. However, for a mining district, the more logical meaning is the past tense of "to cleave," to smash. This is her preferred form of brutality as she fights in the 74th Hunger Games. Ironically, Thresh kills her in this exact method by cleaving in her head.

Coriolanus Snow

The legendary Roman leader is most famous because of Shakespeare's play, *Coriolanus*. The play opens with rioting because Gaius Marcius Coriolanus is withholding grain from the starving citizens. He feels the lower-class farm workers don't deserve the grain because they're not in the military:

> First Citizen: You are all resolved rather to die than to famish?
> All: Resolved, resolved.
> First Citizen: First, you know Caius Marcius [Coriolanus] is chief enemy to the people.
> All: We know't, we know't.
> First Citizen: Let us kill him, and we'll have corn at our own price. Is't a verdict? (I.i.3-8)

This might be citizens of Panem's districts demanding food and justice.

After a great victory in battle, Coriolanus becomes ruling Consul. But at his appointment, the tribune Brutus reveals how Coriolanus insulted the people before. He adds:

> You speak o' the people,
> As if you were a god to punish, not
> A man of their infirmity.
> [in other words, a man as mortal and fallible as they are]
> (III.i.103-105).

Coriolanus' mother, Veturia, pleads for him to spare Rome

Again, here is Snow, the monstrous tyrant. Coriolanus flies into a rage and gives a mighty speech of how the patricians (aristocrats) should rule over the lower classes in every way. Allowing the farmers into the senate at all is allowing "the crows to peck the eagles" (III.i.172). In disgust, Coriolanus declares war on his birth city of Rome, willing to kill his own people for vengeance.

Shakespeare makes Coriolanus a completely contemptible figure, so selfish and vile that he'll kill his own citizens rather than let them have a vote. At the same time, Shakespeare doesn't encourage us to understand the character, who only has one weak soliloquy in the entire play. He is no more the hero than Snow is—he's a thoroughly despicable figure who exists only to terrorize the citizens. Eventually, as with President Snow, the Romans execute him for his treachery.

Plutarch, Shakespeare's main source, also wrote about this famous general's flaws:

> Coriolanus...first of all attacked the whole body of his countrymen, though only one portion of them had done him any wrong, while the other, the better and nobler portion, had actually suffered, as well as sympathized, with him. And, secondly, by the obduracy with which he resisted numerous embassies and supplications, addressed in propitiation of his single anger and offence, he showed that it had been to destroy and overthrow, not to recover and regain his country, that he had excited bitter and implacable hostilities against it. ("Comparison")

Here is President Snow, willing to starve the lower classes and execute their children because of a revolution far in the past. Further, he brutalizes the districts, shooting people in District Eleven, sending in cruel taskmasters to District Twelve. By attacking his own people, loyal and disloyal, he ignites his entire country into revolution. His devotion to vengeance, cruelty, and deprivation leads to his execution.

Arrow notes that "'SNOW' was the codename of a Welsh mole during World War II, who specialized in bugging his enemies" as Snow does and that "Colloquially, 'to snow' someone is to intentionally deceive, double-cross, or con them." Actual snow is of course frigid and can kill, in the same way katniss can nourish. Snow is the enemy of food plants, flowers, harvests, and growth, though it does far less to inconvenience those living in cities.

Cray

Former Head Peacekeeper of District Twelve and a corrupt bully. He is likely named for the shrimpy animals called crayfish, suggesting that he may be from the more rural districts.

Cressida

This heroine of the Trojan War, featured in Shakespeare's *Troilus and Cressida*, is best known for betraying her people after she fell in love with one of their enemies. She spends the play using clever banter and witty speech to charm people. It seems appropriate that in Panem, Cressida is a traitor to the Capitol who joins the rebels and directs Katniss's propaganda spots.

Dalton

Farmer who escapes to District Thirteen from District Ten and advises Katniss.

Darius

Darius is actually not a Roman name, but a Persian one. King Darius the Great (who lived about 500 years before Caesar and his friends) ruled about fifty million people in the largest empire the world had seen. While King Darius didn't battle the Romans, they would have considered him an enemy as he did fight with their ancestors, the Greeks. His descendent Darius III's repeated battles against Alexander the Great's Empire and Darius's humiliating defeat are detailed

in *Plutarch's Lives*.

Darius the Great was a lawgiver and builder of roads, creator of a new tax system. Here is the link with Darius the Peacekeeper, fair and just enforcer of District Twelve's laws.

King Darius believed that monarchy was "the rule of the very best man in the whole state," as he stated in his autobiography, and believed in the power of government under one man (Shahbazi). Katniss's friend technically supports the monarchy in Panem as a Capitol employee. The Capitol turns on him for his fairness nonetheless.

Delly Cartwright

Her nickname makes her seem harmless and childlike, like Annie. It's also a very countrified nature name, as "dell" means a small wooded valley. Delly could also be short for several names, most obviously Delilah. In the Bible, Delilah was the seductress who betrayed and murdered her lover Samson by coaxing him to tell her the secret of his immense strength. In District Thirteen, it's Delly's job to persuade Peeta to give up his psychotic rages, though she acts with far kinder motives than Delilah's. Still, she's brought in to charm Peeta and convince him to let his guard down, offering a possible link between the names. Her last name of course means a builder of carts, an occupation suggesting the districts with their low technology.

Eddy

Wounded child Katniss meets in District Eight.

Effie Trinket

"Effie" is short for the Roman Euphemia, meaning "well spoken," a name popular in the nineteenth century (Hanks and Hodges 97). Saint Euphemia was martyred for her defiance of Rome and her secret allegiance to the Christian faith, while Effie Trinket only survives the series by being believed to be a rebel. Euphemia was even thrown into the Roman arena because she refused to participate in the Roman sacrifices, although Effie didn't share that particular problem, sacrificing the District Twelve Tributes each year.

After the Roman Euphemia was sainted, she became known for one miracle in particular: The Council of Chalcedon in 451 AD was deadlocked on issues of what should be canon in the Christian faith. At last, their patriarch suggested that both sides write their beliefs and leave them in the sealed tomb of their patron saint Euphemia. When they opened the tomb three days later, one side's scroll was clutched in Euphemia's right hand (Butler and Burns 142-143). Such a miracle of choosing lots is echoed in Effie Trinket, who draws the lots for the Hunger Games each year.

And Effie is indeed a "trinket"—a frivolous little unimportant person in her own way. Her obsession with irrelevant things like schedules and manners makes her a laughable character. However, most Capitol citizens don't diminutize their names the way "Effie" does. And at book's end she survives by distancing herself from the Capitol. Perhaps her nonRoman sounding name saved her!

Enobaria

Enobaria is the outsider of the Games: testing Katniss, watching everyone and making acerbic comments. She never appears protecting siblings or friends, instead fighting only for herself. Arrow identifies this name as a female form of "Enobarbus," a character in Shakespeare's *Antony and Cleopatra*. After Caesar's assassination, Mark Antony allied with Octavian, Caesar's nephew and heir. However, as they divided the Roman Empire, Antony fell in love with Cleopatra of Egypt and the pair rebelled against Octavian and were crushed. Enobarbus, Antony's best friend and lieutenant in the play, is an outsider, since he isn't bound by the main character's overpowering emotions. "He can reason in situations when Antony's sense of reason deserts him...he is not blinded, as Antony is, by an all-consuming infatuation with Cleopatra" (Bellman 68). He's a commentator who sees what the politicians are doing without participating in it. "He is a cynic of sorts, whom neither power nor love impresses" (Bellman 68). Here is Enobaria, who votes to continue the Hunger Games "almost indifferently" (*M* 369). Unbound by sympathy for the Tributes like Annie and Peeta or loyalty to the Capitol she once defended, she merely observes that they deserve "a taste of their own medicine" (*M* 369).

The historical figure from whom Shakespeare's character is derived, Gnaeus Domitius Ahenobarbus, opposed Julius Caesar's ascent to power and fought him alongside Pompey the Great. Caesar pardoned him, and Ahenobarbus repaid this generosity by allying himself with Brutus to murder his friend Caesar. Ahenobarbus and Brutus allied to battle Antony and Octavian's joint force at the Battle of Philippi (it's no accident that Brutus is Enobaria's fellow Tribute in the Quarter Quell). After Brutus and his allies lost, Ahenobarbus reconciled with Antony and served as one of his governors…but then deserted Antony to ally himself with Antony's enemy Octavian. Antony was killed, and Ahenobarbus died shortly afterward ("Gnaeus Domitius Ahenobarbus").

Ahenobarbus appears a traitor and opportunist, switching sides whenever his master starts to lose. Likewise, Enobaria reluctantly joins hands with the other Tributes before the Quarter Quell but attacks them with a nearly insane savagery inside the Games. In a Game in which Katniss has been counseled to remember that the Capitol is their true enemy, Enobaria is their willing tool, stabbing Beetee so he can't break them out of the Games and concentrating only on her own glory. In the third book, Boggs speculates that the Capitol has set her free, as District Two is an ally, but Enobaria betrays the Capitol before the end. She ends the book dressed in the rebel uniform of District Thirteen, having chosen the winning side.

Mr. and Mrs. Everdeen

Though major characters, they are unnamed in the story, making them feel more like ghostly presences than active, protective parents. This reinforces that Katniss must fend for herself.

Finnick Odair

First of all, to finick means "to affect extreme daintiness or refinement," or "to trifle or dawdle" ("Finick, Finicky"). Finnick does in fact finick with both meanings, as he pretends to be shallow and obsessed with fashion and flirtation. His dainty looks won his first Games for him as sponsors charmed by his beauty bought him an expensive trident. A "finicky" person is "Too particular or exacting; overly dainty or fastindious; fussy" ("Finick, Finicky"). Here is our hero as he styles his hair and insists he's collecting secrets for enjoyment. At the same time, it's all an act hiding his deep unhappiness and desire for revenge on the Capitol.

Sculpture: Finn McCool and his hounds

The syllable "Finn" evokes the legendary Irish epic hero, Finn McCool/Fionn mac Cumhaill. His name, meaning "fair" or "bright" certainly echoes Finnick, as does his skill as a hunter and warrior. Finn's magic powers come from catching and tasting the Salmon of Wisdom, which corresponds to Finnick's fishery. His wife, Sadhbh, had been turned into a deer, and Finn rescued and wed her. However, they only had a short time together until the pregnant Sadhbh was once again enchanted and lost to him. This mirrors the short marriage of Finnick and his beloved Annie.

His last name, Odair, is a variant on Adair and Edgar as they came through the Scottish tradition (Dobson). The name means "prosperous spear," a clear reference to Finnick's trident (Hanks and Hodges 95).

Flavius

Flavius is part of Katniss's prep team, known for his orange corkscrew curls. The name Flavius (meaning blond) was a popular name among many Romans, with one in particular standing out.

In *Plutarch's Lives*, Caesar refuses the emperor's crown, hoping the people of Rome will cheer for him to take it (though as it turns out, they aren't very enthusiastic about Caesar proclaiming himself supreme ruler over their republic). Caesar then arranges to have statues of himself scattered through the city, all wearing crowns as a hint for the people, but Flavius tears them all down in protest. A furious Caesar strips him of his tribuneship (*Plutarch's Lives*, Julius Caesar, 41). Shakespeare's *Julius Caesar* begins with this scene, showing Caesar's greed for power as Flavius is the first to lead the people in a rebellion against the tyranny. Katniss's Flavius becomes a rebel against his will, but his name hearkens back to Caesar's opponent.

Foxface

This tribute is never named within the series, even after her death. Her nickname makes her seem animallike, a force of nature rather than a person. The emphasis on her face and movement likewise takes away from her thoughts and human motivations. Here is the tragedy of the Games: a girl dies and Katniss never learns who she really was. She becomes yet another silent casualty of war. In fables and legends, foxes are usually crafty and sneaky, preferring trickery and theft to direct confrontation. Foxes are predators, but give way before their more powerful competitors and run from humans. Here is Foxface, always taking advantage of the battle between the Careers and Katniss but avoiding a fight.

Fulvia Cardew

The historical Fulvia lived at the same time as Julius Caesar and other famous Romans. After Fulvia married, her second husband quickly switched allegiance from the Roman majority party to the one that favored the common people. His transformation somewhat echoes that of Plutarch Heavensbee, Fulvia's boss in *Mockingjay*. Fulvia acts like a wife or devotee of Plutarch's as she massages his shoulders and echoes his words.

After this husband died, Fulvia wed Mark Antony, and her daughter married Octavian. However, as soon as Antony and Octavian left Rome to pursue Julius Caesar's assassins, Fulvia seized power and ruled the Senate. When this angered Octavian, Fulvia ran away to the outlying regions and raised eight legions to fight in support of Mark Antony's becoming ruler instead of Octavian. This was known as the Perusine War of 41 B.C. (Cicero 48.4.1-48.15.1).The historical Fulvia was not just a

Fulvia was the first living woman to appear on Roman coins.

Roman but a rebel against her Capitol and its leader. All she did was to promote her husbands' power and her own, just as the "calculating" Fulvia in *Mockingjay* (10) pulls strings in war and politics to further the rebellion and Plutarch Heavensbee's authority.

Glimmer

74th Hunger Games Career Tribute from District One. Her name matches her District's fancy goods and her own glamorous appearance.

Gloss

Quarter Quell Career Tribute from District One. Gloss refers to the coating placed on fancy goods but also suggests that his worth is on the outside, unlike Katniss.

Goat Man

The nickname Goat Man, like Thresh or Catnip, suggests a humble practicality and a closeness to nature. While he takes the name of his goats, one goat takes the humanlike name "Lady."

Greasy Sae

A nickname for the cook, invented by Collins.

Haymitch Abernathy

While the name Haymitch was invented by the author, the "hay" at the beginning evokes someone who's rather a hayseed—a country boy with little sophistication. At the same time, its soundalike Hamish has several interesting possibilities. It's a rather rustic British name (suitable for District 12) related to Seamus and James. James was one of the first apostles to follow Jesus, and he and his brother were nicknamed "Sons of Thunder" for their fiery tempers (Mark 3:17). The name means "He who supplants": he who takes the place of another (Hanks and Hodges 148). Haymitch, one of four underfed Tributes from the laughable District Twelve and then a drunken, ridiculed mentor at Katniss's Games, goes on to win at both—he has indeed eclipsed those with more power.

In *Foundation's Edge* (in the *Foundation Series* by Isaac Asimov), the Hamish are the farming community of the planet Trantor after the fall of the Galactic Empire. Asimov described Trantor as being in the center of the galaxy, with an enormous metropolis that houses 45 billion people. Though a science fiction world, it echoes Rome in the glory days of the Roman Empire.

It is the year 12,020 G.E. and Emperor Cleon I sits uneasily on the Imperial Throne of Trantor. Here in the great Multimode Capital of the Galactic Empire, Forty Billion people

have created a civilization of Unimaginable Technological and Cultural Complexity. Yet Cleon knows there are those who would see him fall - those whom he would destroy if only he could read the future.
—Back cover, *Prelude to Foundation*

The parallels with the Capitol and its uneasy President Snow are clear. But after the empire falls, an agrarian population springs up, content to quietly farm beside the ashes of the galactic capitol in a simpler life. They're called the Hamish.

Major Sir Hamish Forbes, 7th Baronet, was held in a series of German prisoner-of-war camps in World War II. He was remarkable for at least ten attempts to escape from the four prisoner of war camps in which he was detained. These included digging a tunnel under the music room (covered by the sound of the orchestra until they suddenly stopped and he was discovered) and making a German disguise in the camp workshop. As the war turned against Germany, thousands of prisoners were marched westwards, away from the Soviet Army. Forbes made two attempts to slip out of his column and finally succeeded on the third, to return to England a hero.

Echoing this feat, *Catching Fire* brings up the question of how Haymitch survived his own game, and Katniss concludes that he must have outsmarted everyone. In fact, he outsmarts the game itself. He plows through many obstacles to reach the far edge of the Game, where he experiments with the forcefield keeping him in, and finally uses it to kill his last opponent. Haymitch "found a way to turn it into a weapon," as Peeta and Katniss note, not just against his fellow Tribute but against the Capitol by making them look foolish (*CF* 202). His partially-successful escape attempt reassures Katniss, reminding her that he has successfully defied the Capitol as she has. In Katniss's second Game, Haymitch tries again, and this time cracks the Game wide open with the help of the other Tributes.

For his surname, "Abernathy" is a Scottish place name meaning the mouth of the Nethy River (Dobson). Over time, its name was adopted by landowners who lived there, indicating their devotion and responsibility toward their land. Haymitch seems tied to District Twelve, as he's especially miserable in the extreme worlds of District Thirteen and the Capitol. Whenever the battles end, he can be found back in his house getting drunk and keeping the doors locked against visitors. His home in Twelve has become a part of himself.

Ralph David Abernathy, Sr. was Martin Luther King's close friend and helper in the American Civil Rights Movement. He helped organize the Montgomery Bus Boycott and several of the major marches and protests. In the protests for civil rights, Abernathy's house and church were bombed, and he endured many kinds of retribution.

In May 1968, following King's assassination, Dr. Abernathy took up the leadership of the SCLC Poor People's Campaign to end hunger in America. This began as a protest by Native Americans from reservations, poor farm workers, and other minority groups. The Poor People's Campaign reflected Abernathy's deep conviction that "the key to the salvation and redemption of this nation lay in its moral and humane response to the needs of its most oppressed and poverty-stricken citizens." Finally, this campaign led to the creation of a national Food Stamp Program, a free meal program for low income children, and day care and health care programs for low income people across America. On the eve of the Apollo 11 launch, July 15, 1969, Abernathy arrived at Cape Canaveral with several hundred impoverished people to protest spending of government space exploration, while many Americans were undernourished (Garrow).

The rebels mirror this campaign, fighting for an end to luxury and technology if the people in the districts starve throughout. Despite punishment, they continue to fight to create a better life for the poor and starving of Panem. In a book called *The Hunger Games*, it would hardly be surprising to find an homage to the man who did so much to try to end hunger for the impoverished in America.

Hazelle Hawthorne

Mother of Gale, Posy, Rory and Vick Hawthorne. The nourishing hazel tree and its nuts are a symbol of ancient wisdom, though Hazelle displays more of a casual pragmatism in the series (Shepherd 244). Hazel is also a protective plant and a motherly plant, as babies were often fed on the milk of the nuts (Watts 183, 306). While Hazelle is the only named parent, she is treated as a dependent, especially early on when Katniss and Gale note that their mothers are like kids to them (*HG* 9). Still, she provides comfort for her family, even in the shadow of her heroic son.

Homes, Jackson, and Mitchell

Typical American/British last names for these traditional soldiers on Katniss' Star Squad. Jackson, a strong female leader and Boggs's second-in-command, emphasizes the capable women seen in positions of power during the war.

Johanna Mason

The name Johanna means "grace of God" and so is deeply related in origin and meaning to Annie, grace (Hanks and Hodges 178-179). Johanna and Annie are cast as opposites, one so fragile and one so strong and determined. In the third book especially, Katniss struggles between these two forces urging her in different directions. Watching Annie and Finnick's happiness, she thinks about her love for Peeta. But Johanna, tortured by the Capitol, friendless and alone, shows Katniss what she could be if she hardens herself to emotion. As Katniss looks on Annie as a younger sister, she comments, watching Johanna, "I wonder if this is what it's like to have an older sister who really hates you" (*CF* 324).

Unlike dependent Annie, Johanna won her first Games by *pretending* to be helpless, and she struggles past her wounds with great determination. She's the definition of power, as Katniss guesses that "She's been tossing around axes since she could toddle" (*CF* 331). Johanna memorably comments, *"They can't hurt me. I'm not like the rest of you. There's no one left I love"* and even offers to rip out the throat of an (allegedly) pregnant Katniss (*CF* 347). Meanwhile, Annie and Finnick are defined by their love and their need to be together, their desire to create a life for themselves and have children, even surrounded by death. In the end, Johanna votes to continue the Hunger Games, while Annie votes no. These two women represent two kinds of strength: one hard and physical, the other loving and emotional. They help guide Katniss as she struggles between her duties to Peeta and the rebellion.

Johanna's last name, mason, certainly suggests a craft (if Katniss's coal district has "Cartwrights," the lumber district could have masons). Masons, like axe wielders, were the physically strongest people in the village, massive and determined, but also quite intelligent and highly trained in their craft. The mason's 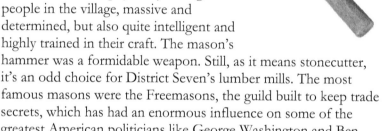 hammer was a formidable weapon. Still, as it means stonecutter, it's an odd choice for District Seven's lumber mills. The most famous masons were the Freemasons, the guild built to keep trade secrets, which has had an enormous influence on some of the greatest American politicians like George Washington and Ben Franklin. This connection emphasizes Johanna's loyalty to the rebellion and the secrets she's hiding.

Lady

Lady, Prim's pet goat, reflects Prim, always gentle, ladylike, vulnerable, and helpful, in contrast with the savage Buttercup. Historically, goats have often been a sacrificial animal, giving us the term "scapegoat." Lady, of course, does not survive the war.

Lavinia

In Shakespeare's (fictional) *Titus Andronicus*, Lavinia is Titus's daughter. She is abused and then has her hands cut off and tongue cut out so she can't tell anyone her story. She is finally killed. This

Lavinia is of course the quintessential victim, so her name is given to the Avox girl Katniss meets in the first book. Though her tongue has already been cut out, destroying her life and turning her into a nonperson in their society, she is tortured and killed. Like Shakespeare's character, she is a voiceless sacrifice used as a pawn between the story's heroes and villains.

Leeg 1 and Leeg 2

Their names sound like "league" or perhaps the Roman "Legion." In fact, Leg. is short for Legate, the Roman word for the leader of a legion. These sisters on the Star Squad are nearly interchangeable to Katniss. Without a single line of dialogue, Leeg 2 is the first on the squad to die, and Plutarch merely offers a "replacement" (*M* 261). They echo faceless soldiers as the Avoxes echo voiceless political victims.

Leevy

One of Katniss's neighbors in Districts Twelve and Thirteen. A levee is an embankment that stops a river from flooding, while leavy is an ancient variation of the word "leafy" ("Leavy"). Both would make sense for a resident of District Twelve.

Lyme

A District Two Victor fighting for the Rebels. She comes from the mining district, and lime is a type of stone.

Madge Undersee and Mags

Both variations on Margaret, these first names mean "pearl" (Hanks and Hodges 217, 222). Of course, pearls are a symbol of hidden value in the story, beginning with Effie Trinket's ridiculously incorrect comment that the children of District Twelve may have unexpected talents because "If you put enough pressure on coal, it turns to pearls" (*HG* 74).

Katniss indeed discounts Madge as rich and worthless, and Mags as elderly and frail. But she's proven wrong in the story. Madge's aunt died in the Games, and her pin goes on to win Rue's trust and make Katniss the Mockingjay. Madge is finally killed because like Katniss, she is a child of the humble District Twelve. Mags too is a survivor, veteran of a previous Game and very handy with making fishhooks, swimming, and scavenging food. She sacrifices herself to save Katniss and her friends.

Martin

The District Eleven retarded child executed for keeping night goggles. A martin is a small furry weasel-like animal and a bird related to a swallow. Both are wild creatures that live in the forest and avoid people. The name also resembles Martius, the innocent son of Titus Andronicus, who is executed as a scapegoat. (The characters Titus and Lavinia from the same Shakespeare play also appear in Collins's series).

Marvel

His district is known for producing luxuries and marvels. This name also suggests that he's spoiled by his parents, fitting as he's a District One Career Tribute.

Maysilee Donner

Maysilee is another made-up name by Collins, one very close to Maylie. Maylie is a form of the English and Scottish name May, referring of course to the spring month. May is also another name for the hawthorn flower and sometimes short for Margaret (linking back once more to the pearl names of Mags and Maysilee's niece Madge) (Hanks and Hodges 232).

The name also resembles May's Lily. May is the time of spring and life, while a lily is the birth-flower for May. It represents innocence, purity, and sweetness, but also death, as it often appears at funerals (Greenaway). And like  the hawthorn, Maysilee brings hope, death, and finally peace for mankind through her mockingjay pin.

Since the name is pronounced "May-silly," it contains another reminder to look deeper to find the pearl-like qualities of this apparently "silly" girl. Maysilee, like her niece Madge, is an undiscovered treasure. Though she appears a helpless town girl, she becomes a fine partner for Haymitch in the games. She is not only deeper than she appears, but she sees below the surface of her environment, dipping her blowgun darts in the poison of the Games.

Her last name instantly conjures a reference to the Donner Party, possibly the greatest tragedy of the American Pioneer Trail. In 1846, a group of covered wagons were traveling to California, heading through a questionable mountain cutoff. Starving and freezing, they were forced to eat their own dead to survive. This grisly story remains memorable today for its tragedy. By referencing this horror, Collins reminds us of the desperation brought about by starvation.

Mr. and Mrs. Mellark and sons

Peeta's parents and his two older brothers are unnamed in the series, suggesting that Peeta, like Katniss, must care for himself without depending on his family for sympathy or protection.

Messalla

Messalla, a member of Katniss's film crew and Cressida's assistant, deserts his home in the Capitol to join the rebels. Likewise, the historical Messalla left Rome and served under Brutus after he assassinated Caesar. In Shakespeare's play, Messalla is often a messenger, a role that switches over to his role of propo director in Katniss's world. Historically, Messalla became an ally of Brutus's enemy, Octavian, after Brutus was defeated. When Octavian praised him, Messalla commented, "Indeed, O Caesar, I have ever been on the better and juster side" (*Plutarch's Lives,* Brutus, 53.2). This suggests that Messalla's joining the rebels is likewise motivated by ambition.

Mitchell

See Homes, Jackson, and Mitchell

Morphlings

The unnamed drugged-out District Six Tributes in the Quarter Quell. Since they have "morphed," or changed, into shells of their formerly heroic selves, they suggest pitiful, helpless victims of the war just like the Avoxes.

Octavia

Octavia, young and fragile, works on Katniss's prep team. She is named for Octavia, sister to Octavian, and wife to Mark Antony to cement the alliance between their families. This echoes how the prep team is treated in *Mockingjay,* as they are kidnapped to help the rebels. Both sides consider the prep teams to be guilty for the sins of their  Tributes, though likely all are as childlike as this trio. They are pawns, used against their will to help the larger political causes. Tortured and imprisoned, the prep teams become victims like Prim and all the other childlike civilians caught in a war far bigger than they are. Venia, also on the prep team, has a name with similar origins.

Commander Paylor

The rebel military leader of District Eight. A rather British last name with no obvious military connections except for one: Army Signal Command's top enlisted soldier, CSM Larry Paylor, was recently quoted as saying the army no longer discriminates against women, but instead chooses soldiers for their skills (Reed). Panem's Commander Paylor is a capable, skilled woman who finally becomes president, and an excellent example of the new equality within the military.

Plutarch Heavensbee

Mestrius Plutarchus (known later as Plutarch) was a priest at the temple of Apollo at Delphi. He became a celebrity in the Roman Empire thanks to his extensive essays and speeches, now known as the *Moralia,* which slyly pointed out the moral deficiencies of those who ruled Rome. The historical Plutarch was interested in moral questions and devoted to preserving free will, much like Katniss's Plutarch. Once famous, Plutarch turned to recording the famous figures of his day. His *Lives* was a famous work of biography, pairing each famous Roman with a similar Greek hero. He wrote on Caesar, Coriolanus, Romulus, Cato, Brutus, and other characters whose names appear in Collins's series (Zalta).

One of his most famous quotes was, "The world of man is best captured through the lives of the men who created history" (Zalta). Plutarch explained that he was not trying to chronicle history, but to examine the character of great men. In fact, his biased writing endorsed and flattered the political figures of his choice and changed public opinion. As Katniss's biographer, Plutarch Heavensbee is likewise trying to do more than record history—he tries to influence it as his expertise with propaganda creates Katniss as District Thirteen's Mockingjay. Both Plutarchs rebel against the Capitol and its beliefs in order to promote their own agendas. Arrow speculates that his last name, "Heavensbee" comes from "Life of Pericles," one of the chapters in *Plutarch's Lives*: "Diopeithes introduced a bill that those who did not recognize the gods, or who taught theories of the *heavens, be* prosecuted."

Pollux

See Castor and Pollux

Portia

Portia is Peeta's stylist and works closely with Cinna. Though the series doesn't state it directly, she is likely a rebel. Historically, Portia was the wife of Brutus and so rebelled against the tyranny of Rome. She also features in Shakespeare's *Julius Caesar.*

Posy Hawthorne

Gale's sister. She, like Katniss, has a plant name, though a posy is just a small, pretty bouquet, suitable for a child.

Primrose Everdeen

The Primrose is pretty and sweet-smelling but won't feed people. On the other hand, it has a variety of medical uses. It's known as king's-heal-all, and is still used today to treat rheumatoid arthritis.

It is also a nice ingredient in hand creams, working as a softening agent (many of those creams also include goat's milk!). Gentle Prim is both a healer and a softening agent herself, rounding off Katniss's rough edges and inspiring affection in everyone who knows her. (Hardy)

The English would pick primroses for May Day (May First, a celebration of spring) and give them as gifts (the hawthorn blossoms of Gale's last name appeared beside them). The very word—with the Latin prim or prime, meaning "first," means the early or youthful rose. Prim is indeed a youthful girl in the spring of her life. This is how Katniss sees her—not a burden but a beautiful flower that she must protect feed and nurture in return for being close to its gentle sweetness.

> Like Prim herself, the plant is cheerful, lovely, and bright, often thriving in areas other plants don't want. It will grow nearly everywhere, turning even ugly little patches of fairly useless dirt into gardens. Prim, too, thrives in an ugly, destructive environment, bringing beauty and light wherever she goes. And, like Prim, who makes herself at home in District 13, or anywhere else she goes, primroses can adapt and grow in nearly any environment. (Hardy)

Primroses were used to protect children, as Prim herself does at the end of the final book, for "no evil spirits can touch anything protected by these flowers" (Watts 304). They were a type of fairy flower, casting Prim as an innocently sweet sprite, like Rue in her gossamer interview dress. Carved into a tombstone, the evening primrose represents eternal love, memory, youth, hope, and sadness (Keister). Memorialized in Katniss's tribute book, she comes to represent all these qualities for readers. Dreaming of primroses meant sorrow and grief, and seeing them bloom out of season was a death-omen (Watts 304).

The nickname "prim" of course suggests proper behavior—Primrose follows the rules while rebellious Katniss does not. This nickname echoes her gentle goat, Lady.

Primroses feature in many poems. Shakespeare, in *The Winter's Tale*, speaks quite to the point of "pale primroses/who die unmarried" (IV.iii.143-144). Robert Herrick in "To Primroses Filled with Morning Dew" casts the flower as a tiny baby, representing youth and childishness. Yet there are other connections here: the Primrose is shown crying and sad (like Prim who loses her sister twice to the Games). And the final line reminds us that Prim's poignant tale will bring a time of peace to Panem.

"To Primroses Filled with Morning Dew"
by Robert Herrick

Why do ye weep, sweet babes? can tears
Speak grief in you,
Who were but born
just as the modest morn
Teem'd her refreshing dew?
Alas, you have not known that shower
That mars a flower,
Nor felt th' unkind
Breath of a blasting wind,
Nor are ye worn with years;
Or warp'd as we,
Who think it strange to see,
Such pretty flowers, like to orphans young,
To speak by tears, before ye have a tongue.

Speak, whimp'ring younglings, and make known
The reason why
Ye droop and weep;
Is it for want of sleep,
Or childish lullaby?
Or that ye have not seen as yet
The violet?
Or brought a kiss
From that Sweet-heart, to this?
—No, no, this sorrow shown
By your tears shed,
Would have this lecture read,
That things of greatest, so of meanest worth,
Conceived with grief are, and with tears brought forth.

Purnia

Purnia the Peacekeeper's name is likely short for Calpurnia, wife
of Julius Caesar. She's clearly loyal to the Capitol.

Ripper

The one-armed liquor seller. Getting ripped is slang for getting
drunk.

Romulus Thread

The cruel new Head Peacekeeper of District Twelve in *Catching Fire*. The mythic Romulus who founded Rome was famous for several acts of brutality such as murdering his twin brother and kidnapping the Sabine women. This Romulus is just as cruel, beating Gale savagely and alienating the citizens of District Twelve. His last name suggests he's from District Eight rather than the Capitol or District Two. This may be a motive for his savagery as he craves the Capitol's approval.

Rooba

The meat seller in District Twelve. Rooba is a type of rural stew.

Rory Hawthorne

Gale's brother. A rather childish name for a dependent.

Rue

 "Rue is a small yellow flower that grows in the meadow" (*HG* 99) beside the dandelions that remind Katniss of hope and survival. The rue is a small, hardy, evergreen plant; like our heroine Katniss, it flourishes in a world of few nutrients. The rue plant was called the "Death herb" as wreaths of it were laid on corpses' necks to protect them (echoing Katniss's decorations of flowers) (Shepherd 250). Its bitter acidic taste created the English verb "rue," to sorrow or wish that something had never happened. Katniss indeed regrets the tragedy of Rue's short life whenever she thinks of her through the series. When she sings Rue's four-note song, she uses it to rebel against the Capitol that killed her.

Rue's most famous literary reference is probably Shakespeare, as mad Ophelia hands the murderous King Claudius flowers, saying,

There's rue for you, and here's some for me. We may call it "herb of grace" o' Sundays.—Oh, you must wear your rue with a difference [for a different reason].
—*Hamlet* IV:v:181-183

While Claudius must bear regret for murder, Ophelia bears it for her losses— for those loved ones like her father who have died in this struggle for political ambition. Katniss echoes this moment when she gives Snow a white rose, the artificial Capitol flower that has always in her mind been linked with blood and  death. Ophelia and Katniss both willingly go to their deaths but take a final moment to give the tyrant this particular gift, showing they know about the deaths that stain him forever.

Granger points out that the rue plant is "cure of blindness, spiritual and physical, that the Archangel Michael uses to restore Adam's failed vision" in *Paradise Lost* ("Unlocking 'The Hunger Games'").

Michael from Adam's eyes the Filme remov'd
Which that false Fruit that promis'd clearer sight
Had bred; then purg'd with Euphrasie and Rue
The visual Nerve, for he had much to see;
—*Paradise Lost* Xi:412-415

Rue the plant offers Adam clear vision and focus, something Katniss gains when she remembers the life-filled child. Every time she thinks of Rue, it's a moment of sadness, but also one of determination to stop Snow from murdering more children. "Katniss wakes up to who she is, the root of her being, in her remorse for Rue" (Granger, "Unlocking 'The Hunger Games'").

Katniss always pictures Rue with her arms spread, ready to take flight, a figure of freedom in a world of tyranny. The rue plant's older Roman name *Ruta* is from the Greek *reuo* (to set free), because this herb cures some diseases and poisons, as Rue herself cures Katniss's tracker jacker stings. It was later called Herb-of-Grace because people sprinkled holy water in churches with brushes of rue (Grieve). Rue's short life becomes a blessing and grace for Katniss, protection in the Game and then a memory of beauty and sweetness through the rebellion.

Seeder

District Eleven Quarter Quell Tribute. This name refers to agriculture. Also, during her interview, Seeder plants the "seeds" of rebellious ideas, as she asks why, if Snow is so powerful, he can't change the Quarterly Quell rules.

Seneca Crane

Seneca was a Roman Stoic philosopher, humorist and playwrite. He said, "A gem cannot be polished without friction, nor a man perfected without trials," an interesting philosophy for the Hunger Games themselves. A bit of a hypocrite and certainly a man with enemies, he was implicated in an attempt to assassinate Emperor Nero. Though he was innocent, he was ordered to commit suicide as a result (Zalta).

Seneca Crane, the head Gamemaker, is of course executed because he is wrongly held to blame for Katniss's defiance with the poison berries. Katniss builds his hanged body for the Gamemakers, reminding them that they too could die for their part in the Games. There are several meanings for Crane, including the bird (which symbolizes duty), but his involvement in television suggests a TV crane—the helpless tool of whoever makes the broadcasts.

Tax

Archery trainer from the Capitol. This city collects Panem's taxes, most notably the Tributes for the Games, who are themselves a sort of Tax. "To tax" can also mean to push someone, and when

Tax sees Katniss can easily shoot the stationary target, he adds more challenges (*CF* 232).

Thom

Gale's friend, who begins mining with him.

Thresh

The District Eleven Tribute who saves Katniss's life in the 74th Games to repay her for helping Rue. "Threshing" refers to beating the stalks to loosen the grain and requires a great deal of strength, appropriate for this massive gatherer of food.

Tigris

The rebel altered to look like a tiger who hides Katniss in her used clothing shop. Plutarch described the Tigris River and Alexander the Great's campaign to conquer the Mesopotamian kingdoms surrounding it—in his histories, the Tigris was where Rome's enemy lived. Tigers themselves symbolize swiftness and cunning. They camouflage and no one knows where they are until they pounce. In fact, Tigris gives Katniss and her friends disguises to help them camouflage among the Capitol citizens. People born in the Year of the Tiger are said to be brave, stubborn, and sympathetic, like Tigris (Shepard 179).With her feline appearance, she embodies the animal nature of the districts, much like Katniss in her Mockingjay clothes.

Titus

Titus was the grisly District Six tribute who resorted to cannibalism. His name links to Shakespeare's savage play, *Titus Andronicus*. In the play, when Titus and his daughter are mutilated and his sons killed, he goes mad. He cooks his enemy's sons into a pie and serves it to all his enemies at dinner. Titus and his enemies finally all kill one another, and a better ruler takes the throne.

Twill

District Eight escapee Katniss meets in the forest. Her name refers to a type of fabric.

Mayor and Mrs. Undersee

The Mayor watches over everyone in District Twelve, making his name literally true. "Oversee" would make him sound too powerful, whereas "undersee" emphasizes that he works "under" everyone in the Capitol. He and his wife are more District Twelve parents without first names.

Venia

 With golden tattoos that suggest royalty, Venia works on Katniss's prep team. Venia (short for Lavinia) was a famous semi-fictional heroine given in marriage as a political pawn. In legend, she's offered to the Trojan Aeneas from across the sea, and their children became the Romans. In Panem, Venia is kidnapped and forced to work as a kind of political prisoner. She is choiceless in a world of politics just as her namesake was.

Vick Hawthorne

Gale's brother. Short for Victor, the next generation that will be victorious and have peace.

Wiress

Wiress is named for her district and its electronics exports: If a man were to be called wire, the female form of the name would be "wiress." She is called "nuts" in the joint nickname of "nuts and volts." Wiress indeed never regains her sanity in the Games and is easily dismissed as "nuts." Though Katniss sympathizes with her, it takes some time before she can work out Wiress's warnings as more than nonsense.

Woof

Quarter Quell elderly Tribute from District Eight. To make woven fabric, yarn fibers are stretched in two directions on a loom. The lengthwise threads are called the warp, while the widthwise ones are the woof.

York

The military trainer from District Thirteen. Field Marshal Sir Charles Yorke was the Military Secretary for the British during the late 1800's, while York is a British city once founded by warlike Vikings (Heathcote 318). The name comes from the term for a pig farmer, suggesting a connection with District Ten (Hanks and Hodges 345).

SYMBOLS

Bow and Arrows

Most heroes wield magical swords. But the heroine more commonly finds a distance weapon like Hecate's whip or most often, a bow and arrows.

Katniss, like mythic Artemis or Percy Jackson's friend Annabeth, has a bow. So do Birgitte Silverbow from *The Wheel of Time* series and Felicity in *The Gemma Doyle Trilogy*. Even Susan in the Narnia series is called "the great archer." Katniss begins the series with the bows crafted by her father, weapons of the forest that, like his logbook, represent her father's forest lore and her hope to feed her family. However, her goals grow from protecting her family to surviving the Games to winning the war for Panem.

The goddess Artemis

In her first Games, Katniss finds a shining silver bow, nearly magical in its strength and power. Once she has it, she knows that she's no longer prey but a powerful warrior (*HG* 197). Katniss shoots to trip the mines surrounding the Careers' supplies, and to slay the unholy mutts that the Capitol sends. She also shoots the final Tribute in a gesture of compassion, a mercy killing.

Silver is the color of moon magic and feminine strength. Its mirrorlike clarity suggests vision and deep knowledge, while the metal itself is moldable yet strong. The heroine's path mirrors this: blending flexibility and endurance, yielding to authority and yet outwitting it through indescribable courage. The silver parachutes echo the bow, like magical gifts from the gods above. However, like the bow, the parachutes can bring salvation or death.

Katniss's black bow in the final book is a bow of death, suitable for Katniss the soldier instead of the young teen charming her sponsors in the Games. It shoots flame and explosives, making her the girl who was on fire in truth, as she grows from slaying squirrels to bringing down the enemy's hovercraft.

Bread

Bread, the source of life, is one of the most potent symbols in the Bible and world myth (Shepherd 253). In District Twelve, a wedding requires the toasting of bread together in an intimate setting. Likewise, when Peeta

gives Katniss two loaves of bread, she regards his gift as an offering of life itself, one she can never repay. Carrying the bread home, she pours tea and insists that her mother and sister join her at the table. They are not starving animals falling on a meal, but a family celebrating a return to life. And of course, the bread Rue's district sends is a source of love and support in Katniss's time of sadness. In the Capitol, even Octavia slips Katniss a roll as an act of kindness. Bread is precious in District Thirteen as well, where stealing it gets Katniss's prep team thrown in prison. All the districts regard it as a sacred gift that must not be wasted.

Dandelion

The katniss root isn't the only important symbol for our heroine. For Katniss, it will always be, as she says, "the dandelion that reminded me that I was not doomed," the single flower she saw blooming in the school yard (*HG* 32). The one she saw in District Twelve when she had given up hope was the first dandelion of the spring, and as such, the promise of hope and a season of food for Katniss and her family. Its tiny flower, blooming even in the deadened schoolyard of District Twelve, reminds her that nature has power even in the ugliest of places. It gives her the courage to enter the forest alone and there she learns to feed her family.

The dandelion is a tough survivalist—it springs up in people's well-groomed orderly lawns no matter how they try to suppress it and hurls its plumed seeds through the world. The fiercely jagged tooth shapes bordering its leaves give it its original French name of "*Dent de Lion*," (lion's tooth) later corrupted to "dandelion" (Grieve). With a bright yellow lion's head, it corresponds to Buttercup the cat and so Katniss herself. It is a small, easily-ignored plant, but, like the katniss root, it is tough and strong. And, of course, it's a useful food source. While it's the leaves that are edible as a salad plant, the dandelion's milky sap has long associated it with milk and nourishment in people's minds (Watts 99).

Forever linked to Peeta and his kind gift of bread, its bright yellow sunburst of a flower glows like a tiny sun on the ground and spreads across the land in a spring wave of brightness. When Peeta remembers that dandelion, it brings a similar burst of hope for Katniss that Peeta has not been lost forever to the Capitol's programming. There is a folkloric tradition that placing dandelion leaves under a girl's pillow will make her dream of her future husband, once again linking Peeta and Katniss's romance through the dandelion that began it all (Watts 99). Katniss calls him "the dandelion in the spring. The bright yellow that means rebirth instead of destruction. The promise that life can go on, no matter how bad our losses" (*M* 388). And this is what they both mean to her.

Duck

Prim is known for her untucked ducktail of a shirt, and Katniss calls her "little duck" in *Hunger Games* (15) and *Mockingjay* (35). While the ducktail shirt suggests youth and awkwardness in the series, ducks themselves are known for resourcefulness as they glean tiny seeds and insects. They also symbolize transition because they migrate and sensitivity because they're very aware of their surroundings. The sensitive, gentle Prim who guides Katniss to grow reflects all these qualities during the series.

Food

Katniss's allies in District Twelve are the bountiful plants and animals, the strawberries and wild turkeys that feed her family. Animals are treated with respect, as Katniss shoots as painlessly as she can and takes all the unwanted parts to Greasy Sae. In her District especially, having enough to eat separates the rich from the poor and defines the main purpose of Katniss's life—getting more. Food itself is sacred in District Twelve—unsurprising as they have so little of it—but it also forms much of their ritual and social life. The lamb stew she shares with Peeta in the Games, the groosling she offers Rue, the blackberries she tosses Gale all bring her closer to them. When she and Peeta see the people of the Capitol wasting it to vomit at the *Catching Fire* banquet, they are truly, fundamentally horrified. If sharing a wedded couple's small scrap of bread is a sacred act, the Capitol citizens are the true barbarians here.

The Girl who was on Fire

Katniss's flaming costume, glittering gown like burning coals, and yellow candlelight dress all reflect the strength and defiance in Katniss's heart. But they also are artificial, in their goal as well as materials. All three are meant to portray Katniss as someone she isn't, from a dazzling debutant in a jeweled ballgown to an innocent girl with no idea of the havoc she's caused. Katniss regards them as costumes, disguises that mask her fear and uncertainty under dazzling special effects. Like the glossy wedding dresses ordered by President Snow and voted on by bored Capitol citizens, they're a reflection of others' expectations for her, rather than her own choices. This is reflected when she's actually burned in the first Games—fire isn't her ally, it's her torment. And though Cinna is trying to help her, he's also pursuing his own rebel agenda.

Cinna has asked to design for District Twelve and seeks to make its Tributes "unforgettable," even before meeting Katniss and Peeta (*HG* 66). And as he dresses her like a doll in all his amazing creations, it's clear they are about him and the figurehead he wants to make her. He doesn't warn Katniss that the wedding gown he makes her will transform into a public strike against the Capitol as ashes and smoke curl around the girl who was on fire, condemned to death in the arena. As she emerges in the gray ash of the mockingjay, she is dressed in someone else's message, not her own. And this won't be the last time.

By the third book, however, she begins to claim her role as not only Mockingjay but the embodiment of flame. She brings down the Capitol's soldiers with flaming and explosive arrows, and then announces to the camera, "If we burn, you burn with us" (*M* 106). She becomes a leader for the rebels, surrounded by the flames of war.

When she's severely burned at the end of *Mockingjay*, she retreats into dreams, into madness, into a cocoon of silk where she feels she's undergoing a metamorphosis. "I squirm, trying to shed my ruined body and unlock the secret to growing flawless wings," she explains (*M* 363). Fire transforms everything it touches, from ceramic to metal. The mythical phoenix dies in a burst of flame and then is reborn, strong and vibrant. In this way, the fire transforms Katniss with "feathers of flame," as she imagines them, growing from her body (*M* 348). She loses her voice for a time as a "mental Avox" (*M* 350) but regains it and finally begins to sing, something she has only done rarely in the series. She also sees that Peeta has gone through his own torment by fire and that they have become the same. In time, she reemerges as a grown woman, one ready to face District Twelve and the love that's waiting there.

"The Hanging Tree"

In the third book, Katniss returns to her beloved lake and summons the wild mockingjays with her subversive, forbidden song. Many fans, upon reading "The Hanging Tree" and seeing the image of Katniss surrounded by the mournful birds, wondered if this moment might be inspired by the war poem "In Flanders Fields" by John McCrae. In an interview at Scholastic, Suzanne Collins indeed related how her father had taken her to the beautiful poppy fields of Flanders, a scene that seemed "straight out of *The Wizard of Oz*"—until her father recited the poem to her there. "O.K., so this moment becomes transformative, because now I'm looking out onto that field and wondering if it was a graveyard," she explained (Dominus). She recited the poem for reporters, who shivered at the haunting words:

Poppy field in Flanders

In Flanders fields the poppies blow
Between the crosses, row on row,
That mark our place; and in the sky
The larks, still bravely singing, fly
Scarce heard amid the guns below.

We are the Dead. Short days ago
We lived, felt dawn, saw sunset glow,
Loved and were loved, and now we lie,
In Flanders fields.

Take up our quarrel with the foe:
To you from failing hands we throw
The torch; be yours to hold it high.
If ye break faith with us who die
We shall not sleep, though poppies grow
In Flanders fields.
(McCrae)

This World War I poem sung each year in Ottawa's national Remembrance Day has several connections to Katniss's song "The Hanging Tree," from the dead soldier who is telling the tale to the poignant request to remember those who have already been sacrificed. Both poems stress that the living inherit the war of the dead, to flee or fight, to remain faithful or forget history's lessons. Here is the image that dominates Katniss's song of "The Hanging Tree," and also the book's final moments, with her children playing in the graveyard to the words of Katniss's final lullaby to Rue. Living trees and flowers alternate with disturbing graves and hangman's nooses. Even among the pretty poppies and larks, there is still this reminder that the land is a graveyard of past battles.

"The Hanging Tree" itself is subversive as it stresses that a man is executed because "they say [he] murdered three" (*M* 123). In the Capitol's world of lies and scapegoating, there's no evidence he actually did it. His lover, who may not have committed any crime, is sentenced to die as well, like the executed friends and families of some Tributes. Finally, the ending stresses that death is the only freedom in their dystopian world.

Granger compares the song to "Strange Fruit," a song about lynchings in the American South, which was used as a Civil Rights song. He suggests "The Hanging Tree" was a rallying call, an anthem of the rebels rather than simply their folk song. Granger hypothesizes:

> The man on the tree singing for his love to join him wasn't a criminal but a revolutionary. His murders were not homicides committed in passion, then, but the shooting of Capitol Peacemakers or Mining Company thugs...In essence, 'The Hanging Tree' calls on the living who love freedom to join the martyred freedom fighter in putting this cause above concerns for their individual lives. It is an invitation to revolution, i.e., to risk death in the hope of a greater life. Mr. Everdeen isn't singing it because it's a simple catchy tune; he's expressing his revolutionary beliefs as openly as he dares and asking others to join him. Mrs. Everdeen, it turns out, was right to be terrified by her husband's boldness. It's probably safe to assume that he and Gale's dad died in a mine explosion that was set by the Capitol to kill men known to be plotting against the regime. ("Mockingjay Discussion")

If the song is a revolutionary anthem, that would explain the strong reaction of Katniss's propo team and Katniss's impulse to sing it for the rebels' propaganda film. Forbidden anthems and songs of revolution have had their place in battles across the world, offering a familiar moment to students of history.

This song also becomes an echo of Katniss and Peeta's relationship as each offers him- or herself as a sacrifice in the Games and begs the other to run. They both wonder if death is the only possible end for their doomed romance, beginning with their attempted suicide at the end of book one. Katniss thinks of the song again when Peeta wants to take nightlock in the Capitol: "For some reason, the last stanza to 'The Hanging Tree' starts running through my head. The one where the man wants his lover dead rather than have her face the evil that awaits her in the world" (*M* 291). Though she resists letting Peeta sacrifice himself, she finally agrees that he should carry a nightlock pill so he can save the mission and avoid torture at Snow's hands. Peeta stops

Katniss's suicide later, telling her she is the only source of hope in his life. As each saves the other, they find ways to keep a flickering hope alive for freedom, even in the midst of horror and trauma.

Holo and Logbook

The warrior heroine often shoots a magic bow, but quieter girls win the day with tools of perception and wisdom. *The Golden Compass* and *The Amber Spyglass* by Philip Pullman feature just these types of tools in their titles, like Coraline's hollow stone or  Meg Murray's glasses, which reveal the truth when the girls gaze through. True vision is a feminine power given by magic mirrors and wishing wells in mythology. Rue takes this role in the first book, pointing out helpful plants and tracker jackers Katniss doesn't notice.

In *Mockingjay,* the Holo has a similar role as it guides Katniss through the Capitol. With its holographic map, it's a perceptive device that lets Katniss see the traps waiting below an innocent-looking street. More importantly, it becomes her symbol of authority, given by Boggs when he entrusts her with command. Using it, she guides her friends through the Capitol and finally saves them with the Holo's explosive power.

Books are incredibly popular in modern heroine's journey tales, appearing in *Inkheart, Ella Enchanted, The Spiderwick Chronicles, The Kane Chronicles,* and *A Series of Unfortunate Events,* among others. Katniss has her father's precious logbook with descriptions of edible plants. It contains a guide of all his knowledge, his incredible forest lore that saves her family from starvation and then helps her survive in the Games. Katniss calls it "the place where we recorded those things you cannot trust to memory," as the notes reveal which similar-looking plants can kill and which heal (M 387). Of course, the book's other great power is that it can be passed on to posterity. As the series continues, she keeps the book and his hunting jacket close like talismans to protect her against the world's evils.

While Katniss and Peeta add to the book in *Catching Fire*, the logbook foreshadows her final book, written as a tribute to the Games and the war that followed. All of her precious memories are recorded there, and not just to immortalize her loved ones. This is also a book with things too precious to be trusted to memory: the message that war destroys the innocent and causes suffering that must not come again. She can pass it on to her children and use it to "make them braver" (*M* 390) and guide them toward a future in which humanity can outgrow war.

The Hunger Games

"In the book, the annual Hunger Games themselves are a power tool used as a reminder of who is in charge and what will happen to citizens who don't capitulate," Collins notes (Blasingame 726). Hunger is the day-to-day weapon used to torture the citizens of the districts "as a weapon to control populations," as Collins puts it (Blasingame 726). Thus, the Games are the strongest version of that weapon, forcing the districts to watch as their children are starved, tortured, and murdered, turned into the savages the Capitol imagines them to be. This is a truly brutal form of tyranny, aimed at the most innocent and helpless members of society, in a theme that echoes through the entire trilogy.

Mockingjay

These tiny creatures have adapted to work with nature, to evolve from spy devices into birds with beautiful singing voices and a talent for sounding the alarm. They, like Katniss, use the power of nature to survive and embarrass the Capitol with their genuine strength, despite attempts to alter and destroy them. Collins notes:

> Now the thing about the mockingjays is that they were never meant to be created. They were not a part of the Capitol's design. So here's this creature that the Capitol never meant to exist, and through the will of survival, this creature exists....Symbolically, I suppose, Katniss is something like a mockingjay in and of herself. She is a girl who should never have existed. (Margolis)

Katniss comments, "I am the mockingjay. The one that survived despite the Capitol's plans. The symbol of the rebellion" (*CF* 247). Indeed, Katniss grows from neglected child into a powerful hunter who can slip into the forbidden meadow to feed her family. Though she comes from the poorest District, the forgettable one that almost never wins, she triumphs and defies the Gamemakers to save her fellow Tribute as well as herself. For the first time, there are two winners, for the first time, a District gives a sponsor gift to a Tribute they didn't send. From her first bowshot into the Gamemakers' conference room, Katniss breaks all the rules. The Capitol, as Katniss thinks, never counted on the jabberjay being able to slip their control, to adapt, to thrive and mate in the wild. "They hadn't anticipated its will to live," she concludes (*CF* 92). Her own will to live and save her loved ones proves the Capitol's bane.

Mutt

While the dandelions and wildflowers, like the mockingjays, are a symbol of hope and nature's will, the monstrous mutts are Katniss's most terrifying and unnatural foes. The mutts, as Katniss notes in the final book, are meant to damage people with "a perverse psychological twist": the tracker jackers bring insanity and confusion, the jabberjays, terror for one's family (*M* 311). The wolves that resemble the slain tributes in her first Game bring revulsion and sorrow. In the final book, reconstructed dogs whisper Katniss's name and stink of Snow's roses to torment her. Worse yet, Peeta becomes a savage shell of himself ready to murder Katniss. These mutts are the ultimate perversion of nature: all are forces of destruction designed to torment and control the people of Panem. In the real forest, Katniss is invincible, but against these misshapen creatures, she has little remedy save to hold fast to her friends and endure the mental agonies.

Nightlock

Significantly, Katniss doesn't defy the Capitol with any of their artificial technology, but with a simple handful of berries. They "glisten in the sun," (*HG* 344), as a shining image of hope combined with the darkness of death. Nightlock represents the final act of defiance the rebels can use to resist the Capitol, like the burning wedding dress Cinna creates for Katniss before his punishment. Far too many of Katniss's allies take this path, as almost all of her Star Squad sacrifice themselves to let her reach President Snow's mansion in the final book.

As far as the word's meaning, "night," of course, is death. In fact, the Latin root "nox," night (along with the Latin "noxa," injury), has come to mean poison in some modern words like noxious (Webster's 975). A "lock" is of course closed and sealed, a permanent state, like death. It echoes both a coffin and the way Katniss can "lock" her special Holo or manufacture it into a bomb by reciting "nightlock, nightlock, nightlock."

The soldiers too are equipped with nightlock pills, named for Katniss's desperate act in the Games as well as the poison the pill contains. And indeed, Gale, Katniss, and Peeta all consider taking nightlock in the final book in order to escape punishment and save the mission. Katniss even explodes her holo with its keyword "nightlock" to save her few surviving friends and end the others' torment. As she does this, she finally accepts that she can't save everyone under her command and must use their deaths as a tool to win the war. In this dystopian world in which even gentle Peeta can be brainwashed into a monster, death is the only thing the rebels can control.

Pearl

Granger notes the pearl symbolizes "genius in obscurity," or undiscovered talent across the world because the precious gem is

hidden within the secret chamber of an oyster ("Unlocking 'The Hunger Games'"). Mags and Madge, whose names mean pearl, both come to embody this quality. By the time Peeta gives Katniss a tiny pearl in *Catching Fire*, she's come to realize that he too has value below the surface. Notably, Greeks and the western culture that followed considered the pearl a sign of betrothal and love (Shepherd 214).

These pearl characters shine like beacons, guiding Katniss to see how Snow's tyranny affects even the privileged, even those who seem witless or clownish: All these people can be heroes in the end. Snow takes all three of these pearl characters from Katniss, leaving her without guidance in the third book, struggling to find the light she craves as it dances on a wall like her flashlight.

Granger quotes the parable of the Pearl of Great Price from the Bible, a story of giving up all one's worldly goods for salvation:

> Again, the Kingdom of Heaven is like a man who is a merchant seeking fine pearls, who having found one pearl of great price, he went and sold all that he had, and bought it. —Matt 13:45-46

The pearl, a circle with no beginning or end, is a symbol of God. Granger explains that Peeta's offer of the pearl is indeed an offer of salvation, as Peeta is sacrificed in Christlike fashion to save Katniss so she can bring about a revolution and a better world:

> When Peeta gives Katniss the pearl before the crisis of the Quell and after promising to die for her greater life, we have the gift of love and light that is only the Christ figure's to give—and a sign of her eventual divinization if she can retain the purification she has experienced there...Katniss's spiritual transformation, even her theosis, is dependent on her "finding herself" and it is this "pearl of great price" she has been given by the Boy With Bread that is her "hidden treasure" and the pure light that will save her. ("Unlocking 'The Hunger Games'")

Rose

Contrasting with the humble dandelion
are hothouse roses, the most pampered
and popular of luxury flowers. If Katniss,
the simple hunter-gatherer, is a cattail
root, Snow will always be the larger-than-
life flowers that fail to provide
nourishment but can fill an entire room

with their overpowering, commanding scent. Worse yet, the rose's
heady perfume covers the scents of blood and effects of poison
that have become Snow's signature weapons.

For Katniss, the smell of the rose will always mask the odor of
blood. In fact, roses have a mythic connection with blood, mostly
because of their deep red color. In the Christian tradition, red
roses are associated with the grail that caught the blood of Jesus,
while an ancient poem states, "On battlefields where a number of
heroes have been slain, roses or eglantines will grow" (Chevalier
and Gheerbrant 813-814). Many myths see red roses or anemones
blossoming from the blood of a dying god. They traditionally
appeared at funerals and on tombs, marking them as a flower of
death like the lily (Watts 103).

Despite the rose's beauty, it has unseen thorns, much like
Snow himself and the Capitol. In fact, there's a tradition that roses
grew thorns when evil first entered the world (Shepherd 261). It
may seem odd that such an adored flower should be the constant
companion of the brutal dictator. But for Katniss, these hothouse
roses are another of the Capitol's mutts, separated from nature
and bred to please the jaded citizens. In the final book, Katniss
enters Snow's magnificent greenhouse where he forces the roses
to bloom out of season in the exotic, unnatural colors of the
Capitol itself. They are "lush pink, sunset orange, and even pale
blue" (*M* 354). Gardens like Snow's greenhouse have always been
considered a symbol of man's power over nature, a palace for
royalty and the rich (Chevalier and Gheerbrant 419). Though the
garden is beautiful, it echoes the dungeons or the Games where
Snow imprisons so many District children with their flower

names. Significantly, a white rose, like the one Katniss sends Snow at the end, symbolizes martyrdom (Shepherd 261).

Snake

Katniss isn't surprised Snow is a poisoner, as she thinks it's "the perfect weapon for a snake" (*M* 172). His "pale, sickly green" skin also emphasizes the connection as he sits dying in his rose garden (*M* 355). In *Julius Caesar,* Brutus describes the tyrant Caesar as an "adder"—a sneaking, snaky threat to the people's freedom that must be killed while he's still a "serpent's egg" and hasn't yet claimed the throne (II.i.14-32). He fears most that power will make his friend turn evil, a threat that takes place in Panem with both Snow and Coin.

Tree of Life, 1892, by Currier and Ives

Coin's first name, "Alma," is Hungarian for apple. Given that a coin has two sides, and that President Snow is often called a "snake," as he sits in his rose garden, references to the tree of knowledge and the tree of life from the Garden of Eden grow increasingly vivid, as Katniss must choose between temptation to give in to evil (Snow the snake) and the knowledge of the true state of Panem and the revolution (Alma Coin). The snake in the Bible is known for telling the truth—but a nasty, destructive truth that brings about the listener's downfall and an end to paradise. Here are all of Katniss's conversations with Snow, whose words hurt most because she knows in her heart that they're true. In the rose garden, as he reminds her she shouldn't lie to herself or to him, his poisonous words change her allegiance and force her to see what her revolution has created. She shoots her last arrow for Panem's freedom, rejecting the two alternatives the presidents offer.

ALLUSIONS TO LITERATURE AND LIFE

Dystopia

> Telling a story in a futuristic world gives you this freedom to explore things that bother you in contemporary times. So, in the case of the Hunger Games, issues like the vast discrepancy of wealth, the power of television and how it's used to influence our lives, the possibility that the government could use hunger as a weapon, and then first and foremost to me, the issue of war [drew me to writing science fiction]. (Hudson)

Suzanne Collins made this speech in an interview, explaining how she used the power of dystopia, or a dark science fiction future, to tell her story and parallel many other famous works.

The novels *Fahrenheit 451* and *Brave New World* both see the future's cities as gleaming places filled with exotic clothes, hovercars, cosmetic surgery, giant televisions, and comforting drugs. The government has taken over independent thought, leaving the inhabitants childlike and naive, rather like the citizens of Panem's Capitol. And like those citizens, the city dwellers have lost the sort of human compassion that would protest sacrificing children, even the children of outsiders, for a glorious week of entertainment.

The books of George Orwell have especially strong parallels in the series and are among Collins's favorites (Jordan). *1984* features a government that spies on its citizens at every moment, rewriting history with propaganda and lies. Television watching and informing on the neighbors are mandatory. Here is Katniss's life, as she's always under observation in District Twelve, even before she enters the Games.

In *Animal Farm*, the pigs lead a revolution to drive out the farmer and run the farm themselves, but soon they elevate themselves over their fellow animals, becoming indistinguishable from the farmers in the end. Here is the true danger of power, and it's one to which President Coin quickly succumbs as she tortures Katniss's prep team and seeks to execute anyone who might threaten her power. The lesson in both stories is clear: Absolute power corrupts absolutely; those who conquer tyrants will soon become tyrants themselves.

History

Dystopias like *1984* are echoes of real-life totalitarian governments, as are the events of *The Hunger Games*. Wiretapping, spy cameras, brainwashing, torture and hunger itself have all been used worldwide to oppress and control groups of people. There are more specific references through the series to World War and Civil War generals, the Battle of Alma, and many military and battle strategies. Collins notes:

> One of the reasons it's important for me to write about war is I really think that the concept of war, the specifics of war, the nature of war, the ethical ambiguities of war are introduced too late to children...if the whole concept of war were introduced to kids at an earlier age, we would have better dialogues going on about it, and we would have a fuller understanding. (Margolis)

There's a particular tie to the American Revolution, with thirteen districts, like the thirteen American colonies, suffering under the taxes and unjust punishments of a distant tyrant. The original colonies produced mostly raw goods like tobacco and cotton. These were shipped to England, where people ate exotic foods and dressed in richly colorful fashions. Eventually, of course, the colonists got fed up with the oppression and rebelled as a single united force. This parallel helps readers identify with the districts, who are fighting for the right to govern themselves.

Mythology

There are several links to Greek and Roman myth, with characters named for Romulus, mythic founder of Rome, or the hero twins

Castor and Pollux. Suzanne Collins explained in several interviews that the Hunger Games themselves were inspired by the story of Theseus, the mythical prince of Athens. Every nine years, seven Athenian boys and seven Athenian girls would be sent to Crete as Tribute for the bull-headed Minotaur to devour. But Prince Theseus volunteered to take his place among the Tributes, navigated the terrible labyrinth of Crete, and slew the Minotaur. Collins comments:

Mosaic of Theseus at Paphos

> My 24 boys and girls who must fight to the death for the entertainment of the Capitol are also called "tributes," like the Athenian youth, and after taking the place of her sister, Prim, who would surely have died, the story's heroine, Katniss, joins the other tributes but is continuously defiant of the Capitol. (Blasingame)

Theseus is one of the great epic heroes of Greek myth. His story is one of valor and battle, but also of traveling into the dark center of the world to confront the great evil within and emerge stronger. As Katniss sinks into depression and drugged madness in each book but perseveres through it to destroy her enemies, she becomes a powerful hero worthy of the classics.

Reality Television

As many know, Collins got the idea for *The Hunger Games* while channel flipping between an unscripted reality TV show and actual war coverage on the news. From there, she got the concept for a game of life and death. She explains:

> The Hunger Games is a reality television program. An extreme one, but that's what it is. And while I think some of those shows can succeed on different levels, there's also the voyeuristic thrill, watching people being humiliated or brought to tears or suffering physically. And that's what I find very disturbing. There's this potential for desensitizing the audience so that when they see real tragedy playing out on

the news, it doesn't have the impact it should. It all just blurs into one program. (Hudson)

Americans have become addicted to reality shows, especially those that make people suffer through the deliberate tortures of *Fear Factor* or the high-pressure environment of *Big Brother.*

Many times, Katniss longs to remind the unfeeling citizens of the Capitol that she's been sentenced to die and that her pain shouldn't be exploited for their entertainment. She shoots at the Gamemakers and drapes Rue in flowers, emphasizing at every moment that she is a person, not a playing piece. However, as she's given a celebrity makeover and a Miss America style interview, as she embarks on her Victory Tour talk show circuit and as she's thrust into the kill-or-be-killed arena with its artificial rewards, deliberately placed traps, and echoes of *Survivor*, it becomes clear she's stuck in reality TV.

When Katniss arrives at the Capitol, she's groomed for a beauty pageant to impress the sponsors. With Rue in a fairy dress and Glimmer looking sexy and provocative, the scene echoes the children's beauty pageants heavily criticized in our society for their artifice and exploitation. Likewise, Katniss's romance with Peeta is all for the cameras and the sponsors, as she notes that she's "got to give the audience something more to care about. Star-crossed lovers desperate to get home together" (*HG* 261). After the Games, the public's adoration becomes an increasing weight as Katniss must perform in her celebrity romance.

Her status as public icon only grows. In *Catching Fire,* bored Capitol citizens vote on her wedding dresses like internet groupies, and Katniss is expected to develop a frivolous "talent," emphasizing again the Miss America connection. At last, she agrees to become the Mockingjay, using her celebrity status to change her world and driving the media presence instead of being controlled by it.

Rome

In *Mockingjay,* the ex-Head Gamemaker Plutarch Heavensbee describes the Capitol's obsession with "*Panem et Circenses*" (*M* 223). In Rome, the citizens were glutted with "Bread and Circuses"—

food and entertainment—so they'd care nothing about who ruled or how outsiders were treated. By naming her world Panem, Collins stresses how her world mirrors ancient Rome—the Capitol kept overfed and swaddled in luxuries, while the outlying districts scream for revolution.

This historical Plutarch, one of Collins's main sources, describes Rome as the all-powerful leader of the world...rather like America today. Rome was the center of culture and scientific advancement, but it was also known for conquering the world and ruling its outlying countries with callousness. Collins comments:

> Once the "Hunger Games" story takes off, I actually would say that the historical figure of Spartacus really becomes more of a model for the arc of the three books, for Katniss....[He] was a gladiator who broke out of the arena and led a rebellion against an oppressive government that led to what is called the Third Servile War. He caused the Romans quite a bit of trouble. And, ultimately, he died. (Margolis)

Like most of her other Roman references, Collins's version of the story of Spartacus came from Plutarch's work (Blasingame 726). While he had limited power as a single rebellious slave, Spartacus became an icon for all those seeking freedom in an unjust world. As Collins names the Capitol citizens after Romans, she emphasizes their spoiled decadent nature, poised on the edge of their empire collapsing. She also reminds us of the precarious nature of our own society.

Shakespeare

Shakespeare's *Julius Caesar* provides interesting echoes with Collins's epic. The story is simple: Caesar tries to crown himself Emperor of the Roman Republic, so a band of rebels conspire to murder him. "President" Snow, despite his democratic title, is likewise absolute dictator of Panem. However, as with *Julius Caesar,* destroying the dictator only leads to more wars. There is more loss than triumph for both sides: Caesar is assassinated, yet the rebels die as well. Characters from the play that appear in Collins's trilogy include Caesar and his wife (Cal)Purnia, and rebels Cinna, Portia, Flavius, and Messalla. (Brutus and Cato are also rebels in *Julius Caesar,* but are remade as Career Tributes because of other connections with their Roman counterparts).

Caesar's Death

In the play, Brutus murders his ally and leader Caesar to save his republic, echoing Katniss's final shot of the war. The rebels also wonder whether they should slay Caesar's ally Mark Antony, echoing the questionable decisions of executing Tributes, prep teams, and other noncombatants. In fact, they spare Antony, who pledges loyalty to Brutus the rebel leader and says all he needs to say to charm him. He then betrays Brutus and publically calls for his death, just as Katniss charms Coin and says what she must so she can end the war on her terms. Brutus comments that he thinks it "cowardly and vile" to commit suicide "for fear of what might fall" but ultimately kills himself rather than submit to the shame of punishment (V.i.112-113). Katniss tries suicide for just this reason, fear of the consequences, but gentle Peeta stops her.

Themes of *Julius Caesar* include the question of when a revolution is necessary and the transience of power: The play starts with one citizen reminding his friends that they all once

VALERIE ESTELLE FRANKEL

cheered Pompey, the previous leader of Rome, and now they cheer Caesar "that comes in triumph over Pompey's blood" (I:i:53). Blood and bleeding, in fact, are mentioned a whopping *forty* times in the play, linking once again to President Snow and the violence of rebellion. There's also a great emphasis on how speeches and public proclamations can gain the people's sympathy, as Caesar orders his statues draped with crowns and the rebels try to win over the people with cries of "Liberty! Freedom! Tyranny is dead!" after their brutal deed (III.i.86). The crowd is swayed by Brutus's impassioned defense, and then swayed again by Antony's inflammatory speech, emphasizing the extraordinary power of the media. This echoes Katniss's television propos as the beloved Mockingjay.

In Shakespeare's sequel, *Antony and Cleopatra,* Mark Antony takes over Egypt, falls for Cleopatra, and rebels against Rome. He loses, and Antony and Cleopatra die together in a manner reminiscent of Katniss and Peeta's attempt with nightlock berries.

Antony's wife and political pawn, Octavia, and his treacherous aide, Enobarbus (Enobaria) are cast in *The Hunger Games* series, as are title characters from Shakespeare's other Roman plays, *Troilus and Cressida, Coriolanus,* and *Titus Andronicus.* These literary references to all of Shakespeare's Roman plays tie *The Hunger Games* to the decadence and violence of the Roman Empire, where spoiled citizens dined on fancy imported foods and watched slaves die in the arena for

Julius Caesar Relief, Folger Shakespeare Library

entertainment. They also connect to Shakespeare's themes as Katniss watches her world cycle through war after war and mourns that all the deaths have changed nothing.

FINAL THOUGHTS

All of these names offer insights into Katniss's perception of those around her, from humble Peeta to stormy Gale. The Romans are treacherous and cruel, valuing those of the Capitol over the less fortunate. Finnick is a seafaring hero, Effie a little trinket of a person. Those Katniss loves are flowers and hardy food plants, filled with the same will to live that characterizes her beloved mockingjay, herself. Collins, too, slips her background into the series, casting military commanders and literary characters into a web of betrayal, courage, and revolution. The Capitol, like its mirror, Rome, offers the same traitors and loyalists found in Plutarch and Shakespeare's classic retellings. In the end, all these characters unite to shape Katniss into an identity born of war and fire.

NAMES BY ORIGIN

American/British names
Annie, Bonnie, Bristel, Cecilia, Dalton, Delly Cartwright, Eddy, Effie Trinket, Haymitch Abernathy, Homes, Jackson, Johanna Mason, Madge, Mags, Martin, Maysilee Donner, Mitchell, Commander Paylor, Rory Hawthorne, Thom, Vick Hawthorne, York

Craft and district names
Annie Cresta, Beetee, Cashmere, Chaff, Clove, Delly Cartwright, Finnick Odair, Glimmer, Gloss, Goat Man, Johanna Mason, Leevy, Lyme, Marvel, Ripper, Romulus Thread, Rooba, Seeder, Tax, Thresh, Twill, Wiress, Woof

Names invented by Collins
Avox, Finnick Odair, Greasy Sae, Haymitch Abernathy, Leeg 1 and 2, Leevy, Lyme, Maysilee Donner, Morphlings, Peeta Mellark

Historical and Military names
Alma Coin, Boggs, Darius, Gale Hawthorne, Haymitch Abernathy, Johanna Mason, Leeg 1 and 2, Maysilee Donner, Commander Paylor, Coriolanus Snow, York

Nature names
Annie Cresta, Blight, Buttercup, Chaff, Cray, Delly Cartwright, Foxface, Gale Hawthorne, Goat Man, Hazelle Hawthorne, Katniss Everdeen, Martin, Mockingjay, Posy Hawthorne, Primrose Everdeen, Rue, Coriolanus Snow, Tigris

Roman names
> Atala, Doctor Aurelius, Brutus, Caesar Flickerman, Castor, Cato, Cinna, Claudius Templesmith, Coriolanus Snow, Cressida, Effie Trinket, Enobaria, Flavius, Fulvia, Lavinia, Leeg 1 and 2, Messalla, Octavia, Plutarch Heavensbee, Pollux, Portia, Purnia, Romulus Thread, Seneca Crane, Titus, Venia

Names from Plutarch
> Brutus, Caesar Flickerman, Cato, Castor, Cinna, Claudius Templesmith, Coriolanus Snow, Darius, Enobaria, Flavius, Fulvia, Messalla, Octavia, Pollux, Portia, Purnia, Romulus Thread, Seneca Crane, Tigris, Venia

Names from Shakespeare

> *Antony and Cleopatra*
> Enobaria, Octavia

> *Coriolanus*
> Coriolanus Snow

> *Julius Caesar*
> Brutus, Caesar Flickerman, Cato, Cinna, Claudius Templesmith, Flavius, Messalla, Portia, Purnia

> *Titus Andronicus*
> Lavinia, Martin, Titus

> *Troilus and Cressida*
> Cressida

DISTRICTS AND THEIR PRODUCTS

District One: Luxury Goods
District Two: Stone (also the Peacekeeper force, weapons, and other defense)
District Three: Electronics
District Four: Fishing
District Five: Power
District Six: Transportation
District Seven: Lumber
District Eight: Clothing and Textiles
District Nine: Grain
District Ten: Livestock
District Eleven: Agriculture
District Twelve: Coal
District Thirteen: Nuclear Energy (reported as Graphite)

WORKS CITED

Aerts, R. "The Advantages of Being Evergreen." *Trends in Ecology & Evolution* 10:10 (1995): 402–407.

Apollodorus. *The Library*. Trans. Sir James George Frazer. Loeb Classical Library Volumes 121 & 122. Cambridge, MA: Harvard University Press, 1921.

Arrow, V. "A Complete Etymology of Names in Panem," 12 May 2011. Blog Entry. http://aimmyarrowshigh.livejournal.com/61131.html#A.

Asimov, Isaac. Back Cover Summary. *Prelude to Foundation*. USA: Doubleday, 1988.

"Atalanta." *The Theoi Project*. Web. http://www.theoi.com/Heroine/Atalanta.html.

Barkmeier, Steve. "The Meaning of Prim's Cat & Kat-niss: Mockingjay Discussion Point 27." *Hogwarts Professor: Thoughts for Serious Readers*. September 4, 2010. Blog Post. http://www.hogwartsprofessor.com.

Bellman, James F. and Kathryn. "Enobarbus." *Antony and Cleopatra Notes*. Lincoln, NB: Cliffs Notes, 1994.

Bennett, Harold. *Cinna and His Times: A Critical and Interpretive Study of Roman History during the Period 87–84 BC*. Menasha, WI: The Collegiate Press, 1923.

Blasingame, James, and Suzanne Collins. "An Interview With Suzanne Collins." *Journal of Adolescent & Adult Literacy* 52.8 (2009): 726-727. *Academic Search Complete.* EBSCO. Web. 2 Sept. 2011.

Butler, Alban and Paul Burns. *Butler's Lives of the Saints.* Great Britain: Burns and Oates, 2000.

Chevalier, Jean and Alain Gheerbrant. *A Dictionary of Symbols.* Trans. John Buchanan-Brown. Oxford: Blackwell, 1994.

Cicero. *The Orations of Marcus Tullius Cicero.* Trans. C. D. Yonge. London: George Bell & Sons, 1903. *The Perseus Digital Library.* Web. http://www.perseus.tufts.edu.

Collins, Suzanne. *Catching Fire.* New York: Scholastic Press, 2009.
—. *The Hunger Games.* New York: Scholastic Press, 2008.
—. *Mockingjay.* New York: Scholastic Press, 2010.

"Crotus." *The Theoi Project.* Web. http://www.theoi.com/Georgikos/SatyrosKrotos.html.

Dobson, David. *The Scottish Surnames of Colonial America.* Baltimore, Maryland: Genealogical Publishing Co., 2003.

Dominus, Susan. "Suzanne Collins's War Stories for Kids." *The New York Times.* 8 April 2011: MM30.

Dover, Major Victor. *The Sky Generals.* USA: Littlehampton Book Services Ltd., 1981.

"Finick, Finicky." *Webster's New World Dictionary of the American Language, Second College Edition.* 1986. Print.

Frankel, Valerie Estelle. *From Girl to Goddess: The Heroine's Journey in Myth and Legend.* USA: McFarland and Co., 2010.

Garrow, David. *The Walking City: The Montgomery Bus Boycott, 1955-1956*. USA: Carlson, 1989.

"Gnaeus Domitius Ahenobarbus." *Encyclopædia Britannica Online*. Encyclopædia Britannica Inc., 2012. Web. http://www.britannica.com.

Granger, John. "The Hanging Tree: Mockingjay Discussion 15." *Hogwarts Professor: Thoughts for Serious Readers*. August 25, 2010. Blog Post. http://www.hogwartsprofessor.com.

—. "Unlocking 'The Hunger Games': The Surface, Moral, Allegorical, and Sublime Meanings." *Hogwarts Professor: Thoughts for Serious Readers*. February 22, 2010. Blog Post. http://www.hogwartsprofessor.com.

Greenaway, Kate. *Language of Flowers*. USA: Merrimack, 1970.

Grieve, M. *Botanical.Com: A Modern Herbal*. Ed. Ed Greenwood. 2011. Web. http://botanical.com.

Hanks, Patrick and Flavia Hodges. *A Dictionary of First Names*. Oxford: Oxford University Press: 1990.

Hardy, Elizabeth Baird. "Professor Sprout Goes to District 12 and the Arena: Some 'Hunger Games' Plant and Berry Thoughts." *Hogwarts Professor: Thoughts for Serious Readers*. September 17, 2010. Blog Post. http://www.hogwartsprofessor.com.

Headley, J. T. *Farragut & Our Naval Commanders*. 1867. *MLibrary Digital Collections*. Web. http://quod.lib.umich.edu/lib/colllist.

Heathcote, T.A. *The British Field Marshals 1736 – 1997*. London: Leo Cooper, 1997.

Herrick, Robert. "To Primroses Filled with Morning Dew." *The Poetical Works of Robert Herrick*. Ed. F.W. Moorman. USA: Cornell University Library, 2009, 73.

Hudson, Hannah Trierweiler. "Sit Down with Suzanne Collins." *Instructor* 120.2 (2010): 51-53. *Academic Search Complete*. EBSCO. Web. 2 Sept. 2011.

Hyginus. *Astronomica*. Trans. Mary Grant. 1960. *The Theoi Project*. Web. http://www.theoi.com/Text/HyginusAstronomica.html.

Jordan, Tina. "Suzanne Collins on the Books She Loves." *EW's Shelf Life*. 12 Aug. 2010. Web. www.EW.com.

Keister, Douglas. *Stories in Stone: A Field Guide to Cemetery Symbolism and Iconography*. USA: Gibbs Smith, 2004.

"Leavy." *Webster's New World Dictionary of the American Language, Second College Edition*. 1986. Print.

"Major Sir Hamish Forbes, Bt: Champion of Highland and Gaelic Culture who as a Wartime POW had been Decorated for his Numerous Escape Attempts," *The Times*, September 20, 2007. Web. http://www.thesundaytimes.co.uk.

Margolis, Rick. "The Last Battle." *School Library Journal* 56.8 (2010): 24-27. *Academic Search Complete*. EBSCO. Web. 2 Sept. 2011.

McCrae, John. "In Flanders Fields." *Modern British Poetry*. Ed. Louis Untermeyer. New York, Harcourt, Brace and Howe, 1920, 83.

Milton, John. *L'Allegro. The Milton Reading Room*. Ed. Thomas H. Luxon, March 2008. Web. http://www.dartmouth.edu/~milton.

—. *Paradise Lost. The Milton Reading Room*. Ed. Thomas H. Luxon, March 2008. Web. http://www.dartmouth.edu/~milton.

"Nox, Noxious." *Webster's New World Dictionary of the American Language, Second College Edition.* 1986. Print.

Playfair, Major-General I.S.O.; Molony, Brigadier C.J.C.; Flynn, Captain F.C.; Major General H. L., Davies; Gleave, Group Captain T.P. *The Mediterranean and Middle East,* History of the Second World War, United Kingdom Military Series, Volume V The Campaign in Sicily and the Campaign in Italy 3 September 1943 to 31 March 1944, London: Her Majesty's Stationary Office, 1973.

Plutarch. "The Comparison of Alcibiades with Coriolanus." Trans. John Dryden. *The Internet Classics Archive.* Web. http://classics.mit.edu/Plutarch/compared.html.

—. *Plutarch's Lives.* Trans. Bernadotte Perrin. Cambridge, MA: Harvard University Press, 1919. *The Perseus Digital Library.* Web. http://www.perseus.tufts.edu.

Reed, SFC Anthony. "Gender Issues Generic for Army Signal Command's G-staff." *The Official Homepage of the US Army Signal Center of Excellence.* 3 May 2010. Web. http://www.signal.army.mil/ocos/ac/Edition,%20Summer/S ummer%2000/topwomen.htm.

Russell, William Howard. *The British Expedition to the Crimea.* USA: Rutledge & Co., 1858.

Shahbazi, Shapur. "Darius I the Great," *Encyclopedia Iranica,* Vol. 7, New York: Columbia University Press, 1996. Web. http://www.iranicaonline.org/articles/darius-iii.

Shakespeare, William. *The Riverside Shakespeare, 2nd Ed.* USA: Houghton Mifflin Co, 1997.

Shepherd, Rowena and Rupert. *1000 Symbols: What Shapes Mean in Art and Myth.* New York: Thames & Hudson, 2002.

Watts, Donald. *Dictionary of Plant Lore.* Oxford: Academic Press, 2007.

Zalta, Edward N., Ed. *Stanford Encyclopedia of Philosophy.* USA: Stanford University Center for the Study of Language and Information, 2011.

INDEX

ABOUT THE AUTHOR

Valerie Estelle Frankel is the author of *From Girl to Goddess: The Heroine's Journey in Myth and Legend* and *Buffy and the Heroine's Journey* (McFarland 2010, 2012). Her projects on fandom, called *Harry Potter: Still Recruiting* and *Teaching with Harry Potter* will be coming in 2012. Shorter works have appeared in over 100 anthologies and journals including *Inside Joss' Dollhouse, Illuminating Torchwood,* and *Rosebud Magazine.* Her parody, *Henry Potty and the Pet Rock,* was winner of the Indie Excellence Award and a *USA Book News* National Best Book. Once a lecturer at San Jose State University, she's a frequent speaker on fantasy, myth, pop culture, and the heroine's journey, with many fans of all ages. Come explore her latest research at http://vefrankel.com.

Made in the USA
Middletown, DE
20 September 2015